UK POLITICS ANNUAL SURVEY 2025

Nick Gallop and David Tuck

UK Politics Annual Survey 2025
Nick Gallop and David Tuck

ISBN 9781917109406

A CIP catalogue record for this book
is available from the British Library

Published 2025

Tricorn Books,
Treadgolds
1a Bishop Street
Portsmouth
PO1 3HN

TRICORN
BOOKS

UK POLITICS
ANNUAL SURVEY
2025

CONTENTS

INTRODUCTION

The past year has been one of volatility and change across so many aspects of British political life. A divisive general election campaign, a change in UK government, social instability, economic uncertainty, regional unrest and global conflict have all had an impact on politics, governance, representation, participation and engagement. Students of politics may study these aspects in isolation, yet considering the intersections between political systems, electoral processes, media influence and the effectiveness of representative institutions is vital.

This book is designed to provide an update on key themes and recent changes to the political environment in the UK, exploring the factors that shape participation, party dynamics, electoral behaviour, and constitutional shifts. In 2024 and 2025, questions have been raised about the overall health of democracy in the UK, leading to a decline in voter turnout in some elections, and a growing disillusionment with traditional party politics. The evidence suggests that participation may be reaching a critical point.

The COVID-19 pandemic exacerbated pre-existing issues, deepening voter apathy in some areas, and creating barriers to political engagement in others. The 2024 general election witnessed stark regional divides, particularly in Scotland, where the impact and direction of nationalist sentiment has become more complex to predict. With the Labour government prioritising greater grassroots engagement, there is an urgent need to explore whether the UK faces a participation crisis or merely evolving patterns of political involvement.

The traditional two-party system in the UK has long dominated politics, but in 2024, further cracks began to appear. The 2024 general election showed signs that the UK might finally be moving toward a more multiparty system, with parties like the Liberal Democrats, the Green Party and Reform UK making gains. This shift raises acute questions about the future of UK politics and whether coalitions or minority governments will become more commonplace. The increasing fragmentation of political support, particularly in England, signals a growing challenge for the two main parties – Labour and the Conservatives – to maintain clear dominance. Will this trend continue, or will the UK revert to a more traditional two-party landscape?

The 2024 general election exposed further weaknesses in the UK's first-past-the-post (FPTP) system. Labour's landslide victory could be attributed in part to tactical voting, while many argued that FPTP failed to deliver fair representation for smaller parties. The Conservatives, despite securing a sizeable percentage of votes, saw significant losses in parliamentary seats. This raised concerns about the legitimacy of the FPTP system, which has long been criticised for distorting voter intentions. With growing dissatisfaction, the possibility of electoral reform is increasingly on the political agenda – yet how realistic is this reform, and what might it look like?

The Labour Party's victory in 2024 can be explained by a combination of long-term and short-term factors. Rising dissatisfaction with Conservative economic policies, coupled with a strong Labour campaign focused on regional investment and public services, resonated with voters across traditionally safe Tory areas. Additionally, younger voters, who increasingly support progressive policies, played a crucial role in tipping the balance. This shift in voting behaviour highlights the growing influence of generational and regional differences, challenging long-held assumptions about predictable electoral patterns in the UK.

The 2024 general election was shaped significantly by both traditional mass media and the emerging role of artificial intelligence (AI). Social media platforms, which have played a central role in energising and informing voters for several electoral cycles, were used to spread disinformation, as well as to galvanise support for particular candidates and policies. At the same time, AI-driven tools were employed to analyse voter sentiment and craft personalised messaging, creating highly targeted political campaigns. These developments raise important questions about the future of political communication and the extent to which media, both old and new, continue to shape voter perceptions and behaviours.

The UK's uncodified constitution has long been a topic of debate, and in 2025 it continues to evolve under the Labour government. With promises to address regional inequalities and devolve more power, constitutional reform has become a key priority. However, balancing national unity with regional autonomy remains a complex challenge. Labour's proposals for greater decentralisation could fundamentally alter the relationship between Westminster and the devolved nations, but how far should this change go? Will it enhance democracy, or create new tensions?

Devolution has reshaped the political landscape of the UK over the past few decades, but has it truly worked? While some regions, such as Scotland, have seen substantial benefits, others, like Wales, continue to struggle with economic disparities. The Scottish National Party's sustained push for another independence referendum in Scotland highlights the growing dissatisfaction with the limits of devolution, but has the momentum stalled? Will further devolution succeed in creating more balanced regional governance, or merely deepen existing divides.

The UK Parliament, once hailed as the cornerstone of British democracy, has come under more intense scrutiny in recent years. In 2025, its effectiveness is being questioned, with concerns about its ability to deliver coherent and timely legislation. The partisan deadlock that has marked recent years has slowed down law-making processes, while the growing influence of party politics undermines cross-party cooperation. What role can Parliament play in restoring trust and ensuring stability in a time of constitutional uncertainty?

Recent prime ministers and their cabinets have faced significant challenges in navigating a turbulent political landscape. The rise of factionalism within parties, coupled with the complexities of devolution and global economic pressures, has left many leaders struggling to implement coherent policies. The Labour leadership under Keir Starmer now finds itself having to balance internal party tensions with growing disillusionment among the wider population. This raises the question: how can current and future prime ministers reclaim control and ensure stable leadership?

The UK Supreme Court has emerged as an influential body in recent years, playing a vital role in safeguarding rights and upholding constitutional principles. However, in 2025 questions are being asked about its effectiveness. The court's independence is often challenged, particularly when its decisions conflict with government policies. As devolution deepens and legal disputes between Westminster and devolved administrations grow, can the Supreme Court maintain its role as an impartial arbiter of justice? Through case studies, comparative perspectives and critical evaluations, this book provides up-to-date coverage of the current state of democracy, governance and constitutional change in the UK.

CHAPTER 1
The UK in 2025: is there a participation crisis?

What you need to know

- Direct involvement of citizens in political decisions is not possible in most modern states. Instead, the UK's democracy is said to be 'representative', with elections used to populate legislative assemblies at national, regional and local levels.
- To claim legitimacy, assemblies need to represent the society that elected them. Yet all recent UK governments have been formed based on a minority of popular support.
- Debates around the contested nature of the UK's democracy range widely. While the UK has unelected legislative chambers (the House of Lords) and a dominant executive, it also has strong devolved institutions and well-protected rights.
- However, one of the most significant democratic concerns in the UK relates to participation. With party membership in long-term decline and turnout at the 2024 election close to a historic low, elected representatives and the decisions they make may not reflect the will of the broader population, leading to a 'democratic deficit'.
- Added to this, low participation often means that certain groups, typically those already marginalised or disadvantaged, are further under-represented in political decision-making. Policies may come to favour the interests of a smaller, more active segment of the population, thereby reinforcing existing inequalities.

The 2024 general election became a record-breaking election, but mostly for the wrong reasons:

- Turnout under 60% was the second lowest since 1885.
- Labour's vote share of 34% was the smallest of any winning party in British electoral history.
- The disparity between votes and seats, particularly for Reform UK with more than 4 million votes, was the largest ever.

Fears over the decline in political participation in the UK pre-date the 2020s. But the 2024 general election has magnified those concerns.

Box 1.1 Key definitions

- A democratic deficit occurs when democratic institutions or processes fall short of fulfilling the principles of democracy, often due to lack of representation, accountability or transparency.
- A participation crisis reflects a significant decline in political engagement or activity among the public, such as low voter turnout or declining membership in political parties.
- Legitimacy refers to the rightful authority of a government or political system, often derived from popular consent, through the winning of an election.

What evidence is there of a participation crisis in the UK?

Participation through formal methods like voting and joining a political party are vital for a healthy democracy. Voting allows citizens to shape their government and influence policies that impact their daily lives; party membership offers an opportunity to engage with key issues, contributing to meaningful debate and policy development. Robust levels of trust among citizens – the belief that democracy is transparent and government is effective – are essential for legitimacy. However, on all these standards, it could be argued that the UK has reached a crisis point.

#1 Low turnout leads to low legitimacy

Electoral turnout in the UK has been declining for several decades, with local elections often seeing particularly low participation. The 2023 local elections in England saw an average turnout of just 35%. General elections provide the electorate with an opportunity to shape the UK government, yet 2024's turnout, at just under 60%, is far below the turnouts of the 1980s and 1990s which consistently exceeded 70%. Considering over 40% of the population did not cast a vote at all in 2024, and only 34% of voters chose the Labour Party, just 20% of eligible voters voted for a government that was elected with a substantial Commons majority.

Low turnout undermines the legitimacy and accountability of governments. When only a fraction of eligible voters participate, government policies lack widespread support. Controversial policy commitments, like the ban on petrol and diesel car sales by 2030 that was included in the Labour

Party's 2024 manifesto, were consequently given weak mandates, making it harder for governments to justify initiatives and diminishing public trust in democratic institutions.

Box 1.2 Comparison: turnout in the USA

According to ballotpedia.org, the overall turnout of eligible voters in the 2024 presidential election was 63.7%; lower than the 2020 record of 66.6% but higher than every other election year since at least 2004.

Voter turnout in the USA has risen since the 1970s and 1980s, when it was about 55–60%. Increased voter mobilisation efforts, expanded access to voting methods like mail-in ballots and campaigns emphasising the significance of recent elections all played a role in boosting turnout. While many democracies face declining electoral participation, the USA's current rising turnout bucks this trend. This increase reflects greater engagement, but it also highlights issues like heightened polarisation and concerns over democracy's future. However, midterm and local election turnout remains lower, indicating persistent disengagement beyond presidential races.

#2 Party membership is plummeting

With the notable exception of Reform UK (see Chapter 2), political party membership across the UK has seen a significant decline, especially for the Conservative Party, which had around 1.5 million members in the 1980s, dropping to just over 130,000 by 2024 (see Chart 1.1). Labour has also faced similar challenges, with membership reducing from over a million members in the 1950s to under half that in the 2020s. Reasons for this decline include a growing sense of political disengagement, frustration with party policies, and generational changes, as younger people may feel less aligned with traditional party structures and are increasingly engaging through non-traditional means like online activism or single-issue movements.

Party membership is essential for democracy as it enhances political participation, shapes policies and provides a direct channel for accountability and influence within political structures. Members also play a crucial role in selecting leaders, such as the Conservative Party's selection of Kemi Badenoch in 2024, and constituency candidates. Their input can steer party manifestos, such as Labour's wealth tax policy in their 2024 manifesto which was largely shaped by party members pushing for greater economic equality. Without strong membership, political parties risk becoming disconnected from their base, weakening their democratic legitimacy and their ability to represent diverse societal interests.

Table 1.1 Conservative Party membership 1970s–2020s

The Conservative Party has experienced the sharpest decline in party membership over the last 50 years.

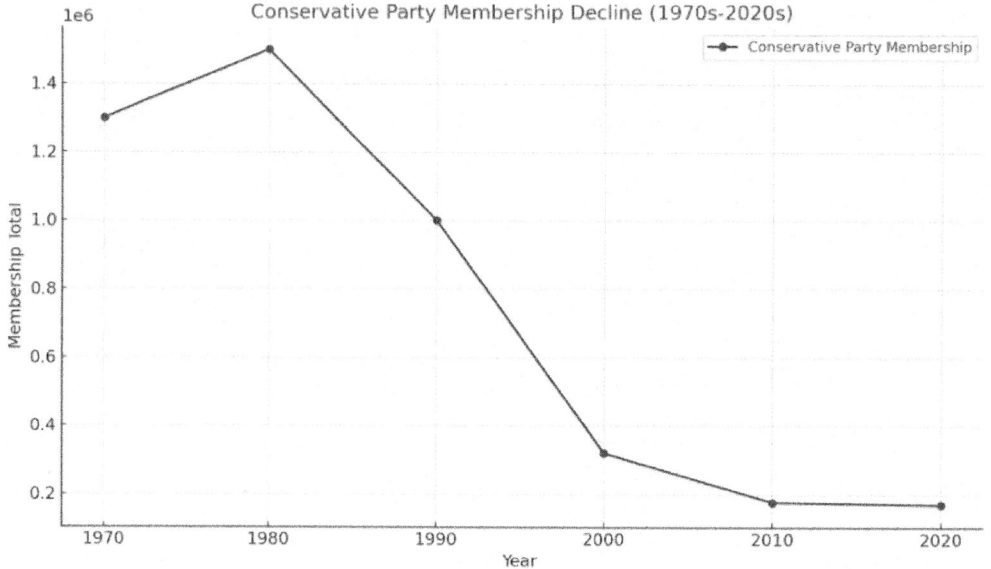

#3 Declining trust; rising alienation

Trust in British politics has hit historic lows, with the 2024 British Social Attitudes (BSA) survey revealing that 45% of the public almost never trust governments to prioritise national over party interests, up sharply from the pre-pandemic period. This decline is attributed to high-profile political controversies and dissatisfaction with public services, such as the NHS and the cost-of-living crisis.

According to the National Centre for Social Research, as many as 79% now believe the UK's system of governing could be improved 'quite a lot' or 'a great deal'. One major issue is that this erosion of trust is fuelling calls for constitutional change, with 53% supporting electoral reform to allow smaller parties fairer representation. This shift indicates that citizens are losing faith in the current system's ability to represent their needs.

Low trust in politics can lead to feelings of alienation and powerlessness, particularly when people perceive that traditional political avenues fail to address their concerns. This alienation manifests as a growing distance between citizens and the political system, leading some to withdraw from formal processes like voting or political engagement. Instead, they might resort to alternative methods, including grassroots activism or direct action, to regain a sense of control.

Box 1.3 Extinction Rebellion

The rise of the Extinction Rebellion movement in the UK in the 2020s can be seen as a response to alienation. The group's acts of civil disobedience, such as blocking roads and staging large-scale protests, stem from a belief that the government is not taking sufficient action on climate change. Extinction Rebellion members often argue that conventional political channels have failed to address the urgent environmental crisis, leading them to 'take matters into their own hands' through disruptive but non-violent direct action. This behaviour illustrates a sense of powerlessness within the formal political system and the need to push for radical changes outside it.

What evidence is there that the UK does not have a participation crisis?

Is low turnout always a concern? Some commentators downplay low turnout. Low turnout at UK general elections has often accompanied elections that have had widely predicted outcomes, such as Labour's big wins in 2001 and 2024. At such elections, the motivation to vote may be less acute, but that does not necessarily signal disengagement from the process. In addition, it is often argued that a lower turnout can lead to the greater influence of more engaged, interested and motivated voters, without less informed or indifferent voters distorting the results.

Is low trust as harmful as it seems? In a London School of Economics 2024 blog, Ben Seyd argued that low trust in government might not be as detrimental as it appears. Research suggests that trust has limited impact on civic behaviour; even those with low trust still favour active government intervention in areas like healthcare and education. Low trust does not necessarily erode support for democracy itself, as most people continue to favour democratic institutions over alternatives. While declining trust poses challenges for political engagement and systemic reform, it does not automatically lead to democratic backsliding or radical shifts in public behaviour.

Arguments to counter the UK's 'participation crisis' include:

#1 Reformed electoral systems encourage turnout

In the 2020s, various proportional representation (PR) systems are used in UK elections. The Single Transferable Vote (STV) is employed in Northern Ireland for Assembly elections, while Additional Member System (AMS) is used in both Scotland and Wales for devolved government elections. These systems have contributed to higher turnout in regional elections, such as Northern Ireland's 2022 Assembly election with a turnout of over 63%, and the 2021 Scottish Parliament election with 63.5% turnout, reflecting greater engagement under PR systems.

Proportional electoral systems are generally thought to be better for democracy because they ensure that the number of seats a party wins is more closely aligned with the percentage of votes it receives. This encourages voter participation, as people feel their vote is more likely to count, reducing the 'wasted vote' problem often seen in majoritarian systems like first-past-the-post (FPTP). PR systems also promote better representation of smaller parties and minority groups, leading to a more diverse and inclusive political landscape, which in turn strengthens democratic legitimacy.

Box 1.4 Global comparisons

Reformed electoral systems around the world have often led to increased voter turnout.

- New Zealand switched to Mixed-Member Proportional (MMP) in 1996, and turnout in the first election under this system rose to 88.3%.

- In Germany, MMP has consistently encouraged high turnout, with 76.6% in the 2021 federal election.
- In Iceland, the use of proportional representation has kept turnout strong, often exceeding 80%.

#2 Alternative forms of participation are rising

The 2020s have seen further shifts to informal, less officially recognised methods of participation. Non-traditional political participation refers to actions outside formal voting or party membership, such as protests, petitions and social media activism. In 2024, the UK saw high levels of non-traditional participation, such as the widespread use of platforms like Change.org and social media campaigns around climate change and inequality.

In 2024, the 'Stop the Bill' campaign gained significant momentum online, mobilising young people and activists to challenge the UK government's proposed Public Order Bill. While this campaign generated widespread support on platforms like X (formerly Twitter) and Instagram, with hashtags trending and various groups rallying behind the cause, the bill still passed through Parliament, demonstrating the limitations of social media activism in influencing entrenched legislative processes, despite large-scale public engagement online.

Box 1.5 Case study: the UK's 'Stop the Bill' protests

The UK's 'Stop the Bill' protests emerged in opposition to the Police, Crime, Sentencing and Courts Bill, introduced in 2021. The bill proposed significant expansions to police powers, including the ability to restrict protests deemed too noisy or disruptive, raising concerns about its implications for the right to peaceful protest. Critics viewed the bill as an assault on civil liberties, galvanising activists, civil society groups and individuals across the country.

The opposition was highly organised, spearheaded by groups such as Kill the Bill and Extinction Rebellion, alongside unions and human rights organisations like Amnesty International. Demonstrations took place in major cities, including London, Bristol and Manchester. In March 2021, Bristol saw a rally with thousands of attendees, some of which escalated into clashes with police, drawing widespread media attention. London protests in April attracted around 10,000 participants. Social media played a key role in mobilising supporters and raising awareness of the bill's potential impact.

Despite the large-scale protests, the bill passed into law in 2022, albeit with some amendments. The protests underscored the challenges of influencing policy through direct action but highlighted the importance of grassroots mobilisation. The events raised awareness of democratic rights, sparking debate about balancing public order and civil liberties in the UK.

Non-traditional participation is crucial for democracy as it offers citizens alternative ways to express their opinions, influence decision-making and hold politicians accountable. These forms of engagement can supplement formal political processes by drawing attention to under-represented issues and mobilising marginalised groups. This broader engagement ensures that democratic participation remains dynamic and accessible to all, even for those disillusioned with traditional politics.

Box 1.6 Is online activism overrated?

Online activism, or 'clicktivism', often falls short of achieving significant change because it prioritises easy, low-effort actions like signing petitions or liking posts over deeper, sustained engagement. While it can raise awareness quickly, this form of activism rarely translates into concrete political or social outcomes. Critics argue that clicktivism lacks the organisational structure, commitment and long-term pressure needed to influence policy or drive systemic change.

Digital engagement can create an illusion of participation, where individuals feel they have contributed meaningfully without having a real impact. In 2024, a petition in opposition to the UK government's Rwanda immigration policy gathered substantial public support but ultimately did not change the course of government action. Despite widespread criticism and opposition – including legal challenges and public outcry – the policy, which aimed to send asylum seekers to Rwanda for processing, continued to progress with limited impact from the online petition efforts.

#3 *Younger people are more engaged than ever*

Young people are more involved in politics than ever, with rising youth turnout in the UK's 2017, 2019 and 2024 elections. In 2017, youth turnout surged to around 64%, driven by issues like tuition fees and climate change. The 2019 election saw another increase, especially with voters under 30. The 2024 election also indicated strong youth engagement, partly due to Labour's focus on social justice and environmental policies. Lowering the voting age to 16 in Scotland and Wales has further mobilised young voters, with nearly 75% of 16–17-year-olds voting in Scotland's 2021 elections. Beyond voting, young people are active in non-traditional forms of political engagement. For example, in 2024, youth participation in climate protests, such as Fridays for Future, remains strong, and nearly 75% of young people report engaging in online activism or social media campaigns.

Chapter summary: does the UK have a participation crisis?

Criteria	Yes – evidence of a crisis	No – counterarguments
Voter turnout	- 2024 turnout was just 59.8%, the second lowest since 1885. - General elections see fewer voters shaping governments, with only 20% of the electorate supporting Labour's majority in 2024.	- Low turnout often reflects predicted outcomes, not disengagement. - Regional elections with proportional systems (e.g. Scotland 2021: 63.5%) see higher participation.
Party membership	- Conservative membership fell from 1.5m in the 1980s to 130k in 2020 . - Labour membership also halved since the 1950s. - Declining membership undermines legitimacy and engagement.	- Younger people engage through non-traditional methods like online activism and issue-based movements, showing a shift, not a decline, in participation. - Reform UK notably bucked this long-term national trend by achieving its much-publicised objective of surpassing the Conservative Party membership figure by December 2024.

Trust and alienation	- Only 45% trust government to prioritise national interests. - Alienation is driving protests and alternative participation, e.g. Extinction Rebellion.	- Declining trust does not undermine democracy itself; people still support government intervention in critical areas like healthcare and education.
Alternative participation	- Online activism often lacks tangible results, e.g. the 2024 Rwanda petition. - 'Clicktivism' can create the illusion of engagement without real impact.	- Non-traditional participation, such as social media campaigns and protests, is thriving, allowing citizens to influence decisions outside formal voting or party systems.
Youth engagement	- Some argue youth focus on non-traditional participation (e.g. climate protests) neglects formal politics.	- Youth turnout has risen (e.g. 64% in 2017) and 75% of 16–17-year-olds in Scotland voted in 2021. - Young people lead issue-based movements like Fridays for Future.

Conclusion

The UK does not necessarily face a participation crisis but rather a shift in how people engage. While traditional metrics like voter turnout and party membership have declined, non-traditional forms of participation – such as online activism, protests and issue-based campaigning – are thriving. Young people, in particular, are mobilising around specific causes like climate change and social justice. The challenge for democracy is ensuring that these alternative forms of engagement have real influence on policy, beyond just raising awareness.

Examination success

Sample essay examination questions:

- 'The UK has a political participation crisis.' Analyse and evaluate this statement. (AQA style, 25 marks)
- Evaluate the view that the UK has a political participation crisis. (Edexcel style, 30 marks)

Examiner's advice:

- When answering A-Level questions about participation, start by explaining the concept of political participation, including conventional methods such as voting and party membership, alongside non-traditional methods like protests, petitions and online activism.

- Recent elections show both decline and resurgence in voter turnout – explain how and why. General elections often attract higher participation, while local elections in the UK historically have lower turnout. Compare voter engagement in different types of elections to assess if turnout suggests a participation crisis.

- Evaluate the decline in formal party membership, especially in the two major parties (Conservative and Labour), against the rise of alternative forms of engagement like online activism, social movements and pressure groups. Discuss whether this shift signifies disengagement or a transformation in how citizens participate.

- Consider whether the increase in non-electoral participation (e.g., protests, issue-based campaigns, online movements) shows that political participation has diversified rather than declined. Compare the UK to global trends and argue if new forms of engagement can counter the claim of a 'crisis' in traditional participation.

CHAPTER 2
Is the UK finally moving to a multiparty system?

What you need to know

- The last century has been characterised by a two-party 'duopoly' in UK politics and has seen an almost complete concentration of political power at Westminster in the hands of the Labour and Conservative parties.

- While inroads have been made by alternative parties into the vote share previously enjoyed by the two main parties, this has rarely crossed over into substantial numbers of seats won. Even in 2010, when the combined Labour/Conservative vote share slipped to 65%, the two main parties still won 87% of the seats.

- Some commentators suggest that the 2024 general election was a pivotal moment in UK party politics. Not only did the Labour–Conservative combined vote share slip well below 60% (to 57.4%) but the third most successful party, the Liberal Democrats, won a record 72 seats: over 11% of the total and just 40 fewer than the Conservatives.

- Arguments supporting a more permanent shift towards a multiparty system, drawing on the success of minor parties in devolved elections and recent UK general election data, are undermined by the frequent decline or disappearance of so many 'challenger' parties such as the UK Independence Party, the Brexit Party and the Scottish National Party.

Are the two main parties really in decline?

The first-past-the-post (FPTP) electoral system has historically entrenched the dominance of the two major political parties in the UK. The system, designed to produce strong single-party governments, disproportionately rewards the parties with the largest vote shares while marginalising smaller parties. The adversarial structure of Parliament, with its emphasis on the government–opposition divide, reinforces this duopoly.

However, recent elections suggest that the two-party system is facing increasing pressure, with growing evidence of its decline and the emergence of a multiparty dynamic. This trend is reflected in three key areas: the steady erosion of the combined vote share of the two main parties, the improved performance of minor parties in translating votes into parliamentary representation, and the rise of new political forces such as Reform UK.

Box 2.1 Key definitions

- Multiparty politics is a system where multiple political parties compete for power, often resulting in coalitions or minority governments. In the UK, the devolved governments exemplify multiparty politics, with parties like the SNP, Plaid Cymru and the Greens playing significant roles alongside Labour and the Conservatives in regional governments.
- A two-party system is where two major parties dominate political competition, typically alternating in power. The UK's Westminster elections largely reflect a two-party system, with the Conservative Party and Labour Party being the primary contenders for government.
- A dominant party system is where one party consistently holds power over a prolonged period, overshadowing opposition parties. An example is the dominance of the Conservative Party in the UK during the 1980s under Margaret Thatcher and the Labour Party's control from 1997 to 2010 under Tony Blair and Gordon Brown.

#1 The declining combined vote share of Labour and the Conservatives has raised questions about whether this represents a structural shift in voter behaviour. In the 2010 and 2015 general elections, the two main parties secured a combined vote share of 65% and 67% respectively, a significant drop from their historical dominance of 75%+ in earlier decades. The polarising effect of Brexit in 2017 and 2019 saw their combined vote share rise to highs of 82% and 75%, but this figure fell to just 57% in 2024. The extent to which these fluctuations suggest that the electorate is increasingly turning to alternative parties, signalling a potential long-term structural decline in the dominance of the two main parties, is open to debate.

#2 *The improving performance of minor parties* is a key indicator of a weakening two-party system. The Liberal Democrats, for instance, achieved a breakthrough in 2010 under Nick Clegg, winning 23% of the vote and 57 seats. Although their fortunes waned in subsequent elections, the 2024 general election marked a resurgence, with the party reclaiming 10% of the vote and a significant increase in parliamentary representation. Similarly, the Scottish National Party (SNP) has maintained a stronghold in Scotland, winning most of the Westminster seats (48 out of 59 seats in 2019) before experiencing a decline in 2024. These outcomes highlight how minor parties are overcoming FPTP's inherent biases, capitalising on regional and issue-specific voter bases to secure meaningful representation.

#3 *The rise of new political forces* was one of the main stories of the 2024 general election. Reform UK, led by Nigel Farage, secured a significant share of the vote, marking a critical shift in the political landscape. Farage's personal victory in winning a Westminster seat for the first time symbolises the growing appeal of alternative political narratives, particularly among disaffected Conservative voters. While Reform UK's overall parliamentary representation remains modest due to FPTP, its ability to attract a substantial portion of the electorate indicates a new dynamic in UK politics, further weakening the traditional Labour–Conservative duopoly.

Box 2.2 Global comparisons

- Germany operates under a multiparty system, with significant parties like the CDU/CSU, SPD, Greens and FDP often forming coalition governments. This system promotes negotiation and compromise to achieve stable governance.
- The United States exemplifies a two-party system, dominated by the Democrats and Republicans. While third parties exist, they rarely win significant offices, and political competition revolves primarily around these two major parties.
- South Africa's African National Congress (ANC) has traditionally dominated national politics since the end of apartheid in 1994, consistently winning large majorities. Opposition parties exist, but few have seriously challenged the ANC's hold on power.

Is Reform UK set to break the UK's duopoly?

Arguably one of the shortest ever government 'honeymoon' periods was enjoyed by the Labour Party in 2024. In December 2024, just five months after Labour's landslide victory came a poll by market research agency Find Out Now which put the Conservatives on 26%, Reform on 24% and Labour third on 23%. Unpopular post-election government policies, especially the means-testing of the winter fuel allowance for pensioners and higher taxes placed on employees and businesses, had not played well with an increasingly volatile electorate.

Box 2.3 Case study: Reform UK's rising support in UK politics

Recent polling by Find Out Now suggested that Reform has overtaken Labour in voting intentions. However, this isolated poll contrasts with broader trends showing Labour still leading by a narrow margin.

Analysis of the 2024 general election results reveals limited overlap between Labour and Reform's voter bases. A negligible correlation (-0.01) between their vote shares across constituencies indicates Reform did not significantly erode Labour's support, particularly in traditional Labour strongholds. In contrast, Reform gained more traction in Conservative-dominated areas, reflected in a modest positive correlation (0.21) between their vote shares.

Notably, Reform's success also came at the expense of the Liberal Democrats and Greens, with negative correlations of -0.25 and -0.27, respectively. These findings suggest that Reform attracted disillusioned protest voters who traditionally supported these smaller parties. This reflects a broader fragmentation of the UK's political landscape, driven by weakening attachments to major parties.

For Labour to counter this trend, it must focus on 'delivery' of its policies, as public dissatisfaction with economic challenges persists. With fewer disruptive events like Brexit or COVID-19 likely in the near term, Labour has an opportunity to restore economic growth and voter confidence, reducing Reform's appeal as a protest vote.

This case underscores the fluidity of UK politics and the growing role of smaller parties in shaping voter behaviour.

Source: adapted from Jo Adetunji, Editor, The Conversation UK in *Is Reform really pulling ahead of Labour? Polling expert on what to really make of Farage's supposed lead* (December 2024)

Recent polling data has led some commentators to extrapolate that if such figures were sustained up to a general election, the Labour Party would lose over 200 of its MPs, with gains mainly shared between the Conservatives and Reform UK. Others reminded that while mid-term opinion polls, using disputed data collection methods, provide stimulating news coverage, they have little to no relevance on distant general election outcomes.

That said, other polls conducted in late December 2024 also indicated that Reform UK could secure up to 120 seats in a general election, with significant gains in regions like East Anglia, Essex and northern England, thereby making inroads into traditional Labour strongholds and attracting voters from both major parties. It sets up the possibility that Reform UK might be set to make significant inroads in the UK's two-party system and several factors present a genuine challenge to the Westminster dominance of the Conservative and Labour Parties.

#1 *The growth of Reform's party membership* certainly succeeded in grabbing media attention in December 2024 and January 2025. A sustained rise in party membership is a potential key indicator of a lasting shift in Reform's political prominence. While Nigel Farage's predecessor party, the UK Independence Party, peaked at 46,000 members in 2015, the headline-grabbing objective of surpassing Conservative Party membership numbers were achieved in December 2024.

Box 2.4 Reform UK – the 'real' opposition?

In late December 2024, many news websites led with news of Reform UK's claim to have more members than the Conservative Party, thereby becoming 'the real opposition' according to Nigel Farage, and prompting a furious exchange with the Conservative leadership. A much-publicised digital counter on the Reform UK party's website saw the number tick past 131,680 members, which was the amount the Conservative Party declared before its leadership election in the autumn, on 26 December 2024.

Nigel Farage, party leader and MP for Clacton-on-Sea, claimed on X that 'the youngest political party in British politics has just overtaken the oldest political party in the world. Reform UK are now the real opposition'. Meanwhile Conservative leader Kemi Badenoch accused the party of issuing misleading figures: 'manipulating your own supporters at Xmas eh, Nigel? It's not real. It's a fake … coded to tick up automatically.'

#2 The popularity of Reform's leadership saw a sustained upward shift in the post-election period. Support for Reform UK had been growing generally since the general election, and opinion polls also indicated that Nigel Farage had become one of the most popular UK politicians since he was elected as an MP in 2024. The Guardian newspaper quoted an Ipsos survey in December 2024 which found that Farage had a net favourability rating higher than both Keir Starmer and Rachel Reeves.

Box 2.5 Support for Nigel Farage – what do the polls say?

- A YouGov survey from early January 2025 indicated that 30% of Britons hold a favourable view of Farage, with 62% viewing him unfavourably, resulting in a net rating of -32. Yet according to YouGov's data, no party leader is seen favourably by more than 30% of Britons.
- An Ipsos Political Pulse survey conducted between 13 and 17 December 2024, reveals that Farage's favourability ratings are competitive with other leading politicians and parties, reflecting his significant presence in the political landscape.

#3 Broad support for Reform's policies is another factor indicating a change in the structure of the UK's party system. On one side of the spectrum, Reform UK has adopted policies traditionally associated with the left, such as advocating for the nationalisation of key industries. Richard Tice, a prominent figure in the party, has supported nationalising sectors like energy and railways, appealing to Labour voters dissatisfied with the current government's economic strategies.

For traditional Conservative voters, Reform UK's firm stance on immigration and commitment to reducing taxes align with traditional right-wing priorities. The party's emphasis on stricter immigration controls and economic policies favouring lower taxation resonate with those who feel the Conservative Party has shifted away from these core principles.

Why has the Liberal Democrat Party not broken through?

The Liberal Democrat Party has long sought to establish itself as a central player in British politics, aiming to challenge the two-party dominance of Labour and the Conservatives. While the party has experienced moments of success, such as its electoral performance in 2010 that led to a five-year partnership in a coalition government, it has struggled to achieve the critical mass necessary to transform the UK into a truly multiparty system. Even the 2024 general election, though historically significant for voter volatility, failed to mark a decisive turning point for the party.

#1 Electoral geography: one key obstacle for the Liberal Democrats is their geographically dispersed support. Unlike Labour and the Conservatives, whose votes are concentrated in urban or rural areas, the Liberal Democrats' support base is spread thinly across the country. This distribution dilutes their impact under the first-past-the-post (FPTP) electoral system, which favours parties with regional strongholds. While the Liberal Democrats consistently achieve a significant share of the national vote – sometimes over 20% – this rarely translates into proportionate representation in Parliament.

#2 Squeezed by the two main parties: the Liberal Democrats are caught in a political squeeze between Labour and the Conservatives. In elections, voters often adopt a tactical approach, backing the constituency candidate they perceive as most capable of defeating their least-preferred option. This dynamic leaves the Liberal Democrats struggling to maintain their distinct identity, as their core policies often overlap with one of the major parties, making it difficult to carve out a unique and compelling position.

Labour and the Liberal Democrats share progressive stances on climate change, healthcare and social justice. This alignment can lead voters to view the Liberal Democrats as an auxiliary to Labour rather than a viable alternative. Similarly, in traditionally Conservative constituencies, anti-Tory voters often prioritise Labour as the main challenger, sidelining the Liberal Democrats in favour of a stronger opposition.

#3: *The 2024 election was not a breakthrough*: although the 2024 general election was marked by historic low turnout and voter dissatisfaction, it did not yield a breakthrough for the Liberal Democrats. Despite increased volatility and disillusionment with the two major parties, the Liberal Democrats failed to capitalise significantly. Their vote share and percentage of the Westminster seats remained healthy but modest (12% and 11% respectively), and their influence on policy and governance remained peripheral.

The election underscored the structural and strategic challenges the Liberal Democrats face. Their inability to present a compelling alternative, combined with the enduring dominance of Labour and the Conservatives, has left the UK political system as a two-party contest.

The Liberal Democrats' failure to break through and create multiparty politics in the UK is rooted in their dispersed support base, their position as a 'squeezed middle' between Labour and the Conservatives, and their inability to capitalise on moments of political flux like the 2024 election. While they remain an important part of the political landscape, systemic barriers and strategic challenges continue to prevent them from reshaping British politics into a multiparty system.

Factor	Yes	No
Declining Labour–Conservative vote share	Combined vote share of Labour and Conservatives fell to 57.4% in 2024, the lowest in decades.	Despite the decline, the two major parties still dominate parliamentary seats due to the FPTP system.
Minor parties' electoral success	The Liberal Democrats won a record 72 seats in 2024, securing over 11% of total seats.	Success of minor parties is often temporary, as seen with the decline of UKIP, the Brexit Party and the SNP.
Rise of new political forces	Reform UK gained significant vote share in 2024, reflecting growing dissatisfaction with traditional parties.	Reform UK's seat count remains modest due to FPTP, and its support base may not sustain long-term growth.

Electoral system (FPTP)	Minor parties are improving at overcoming FPTP's biases, particularly in regional strongholds like Scotland.	FPTP inherently favours larger, established parties, entrenching the Labour–Conservative duopoly.
Voter bolatility	Increasing volatility in voter behaviour, including support for protest parties, suggests a shift toward fragmentation.	Voter volatility often reflects short-term dissatisfaction rather than a structural shift to multiparty politics.
Regional multiparty dynamics	Devolved governments exhibit multiparty systems, with strong roles for SNP, Plaid Cymru and Greens.	Increased vote share and seats in 2024 show potential for growth as a third-party force.
Challenges for Liberal Democrats	At Westminster, the two-party system remains dominant, with limited influence from regional dynamics.	Geographic dispersion of votes and tactical voting continue to limit their ability to challenge the two-party system.

Implications

While recent trends indicate growing pressure on the two-party system, significant structural barriers – particularly the FPTP electoral system – continue to constrain minor parties. The UK appears to be moving toward greater fragmentation in voter preferences but has not yet transitioned to a fully multiparty system.

Conclusion

There is little doubt that UK's political landscape in the 2020s is undergoing a transformation, as evidenced by declining vote shares for the two main parties, the increased effectiveness of minor parties in gaining representation and the rise of new challengers like Reform UK. While FPTP and the adversarial parliamentary system have historically reinforced the two-party dominance, recent elections suggest that the system is evolving, pointing towards a more fragmented and pluralistic political future.

Examination success

Sample essay examination questions:

- 'The UK's two-party system is alive and well.' Analyse and evaluate this statement. (AQA style, 25 marks)
- Evaluate the view that the UK's two-party system has been replaced by a multiparty system. (Edexcel style, 30 marks)

Examiner's advice:

- Define the key terms by clearly explaining what is meant by a 'two-party system' (domination by two major parties in elections and governance) and a 'multiparty system' (where multiple parties have significant influence on political outcomes). Use examples like the Labour and Conservative party's historical dominance versus the rise of smaller parties (e.g. SNP, Reform UK or Greens).

- Use recent electoral data, especially the 2017, 2019 and 2024 UK general elections, and contrast this with regional and local elections to highlight trends. For example, note the resurgence of Labour and the Conservatives in vote share prior to 2024 versus the growing role of regional parties like the SNP or the electoral impact of Reform UK.

- Analyse institutional factors such as the role of first-past-the-post (FPTP) in sustaining a two-party system and contrast it with proportional representation systems that sustain multiparty politics in devolved legislatures like Scotland and Wales.

- Evaluate counterarguments such as while Labour and the Conservatives dominate Westminster, parties like UKIP (historically) or Reform UK (more recently) do indeed influence the political agenda, shape outcomes and indicate a shift towards a multiparty dynamic in voter behaviour.

CHAPTER 3
General election 2024: did the weaknesses of first-past-the-post outweigh the strengths?

What you need to know

- Political processes and parliamentary systems are shaped by the electoral systems used to translate votes in elections into seats in representative assemblies.

- In the UK, activities and procedures in the Westminster Parliament are largely based on first-past-the-post's (FPTP) traditional strengths of creating a stable, single-party majority government and a strong opposition.

- FPTP is not a proportional electoral system. It only requires each constituency candidate to win a 'simple plurality' of votes – just one more vote than their closest rival. A winning candidate is then returned to Parliament from each of the UK's 650 constituencies.

- Other electoral systems used in non-Westminster elections in the UK range from non-proportional ones, such as the supplementary vote (SV) used for many mayoral elections, to highly proportional systems such as the single transferable vote (STV) used in Northern Ireland. See Box 3.1.

The durability of first-past-the-post (FPTP) as the system used to elect MPs to Westminster is based on a lengthy track record of delivering on its main strengths. Just one general election in more than 80 years since 1945 failed to create a single-party government and only a handful of those elections failed to create a government with a majority of seats in the House of Commons. FPTP is seen by many, MPs included, as the most appropriate system to support the UK's democracy and its parliamentary arrangements. It has been used to determine the outcome of UK elections for centuries, despite its apparent flaws.

However, the 2010s saw FPTP at its most erratic. A coalition government was formed when the 2010 vote did not lead to a sufficiently strong winner, and a government with the slenderest post-war majority of just 12 seats was formed in 2015. When 2017 saw the formation of a minority government, many commentators concluded that FPTP's days were numbered.

Yet for supporters of FPTP, the last two general elections have restored its reputation. In 2019 the Conservative Party secured the largest working government majority since the 2001 election and in 2024 the Labour Party achieved a landslide victory. Both of these elections produced strong governments with clear mandates, able to enact their manifesto commitments while being accountable in Parliament by a coherent opposition party.

Beneath those headline-grabbing recent victories however, disparities between votes and seats are as stark as ever. In 2019, the Conservative government secured a majority of 80 seats in the House of Commons (56% of the seats) based on 44% of the national vote. In 2024 the margin between seats won and votes was even greater with the Labour Party winning 412 seats (63% of the seats) from just 33.8% of the votes.

Table 3.1 Results of the 2024 general election

Party	Seats won	Seat gains	Seat losses	Vote share (%)	Change (+/-)	Total votes
Labour Party	411	218	7	33.8	+1.7	9,712,011
Conservative Party	121	1	252	23.7	-19.9	6,814,469
Liberal Democrats	71	64	0	12.2	+0.6	3,499,969
Reform UK	5	5	0	14.3	+12.3	4,117,620
Green Party	4	3	0	6.4	+3.8	1,841,888
SNP	9	1	40	2.5	-1.3	708,759
Plaid Cymru	4	2	0	0.68	+0.2	194,811

Box 3.1 The UK's electoral systems

First-past-the-post is a plurality voting system. Unlike majority voting systems, which mostly require 50% of the votes to win (i.e. more than all the votes for other candidates), plurality voting systems see the most popular choice elected, regardless of how many votes are secured.

Proportional representation describes electoral systems with a close alignment between votes cast and seats won. A large number of electoral systems that are proportional or that have an element of proportionality are used in the UK for non-Westminster elections. These include:

- The Additional Member System (AMS) is used in Scottish parliamentary and Welsh assembly elections. AMS is a hybrid of FPTP and the regional list system giving voters two votes – one to elect a constituency MP and one in support of a political party.
- The Single Transferable Vote (STV) is a highly proportional voting system used for elections to the Northern Ireland Assembly.

While most modern democracies do not use plurality systems to elect national legislatures, the UK is far from alone. In the USA, 48 out of 50 states use a plurality-based system for presidential and congressional elections.

Did the 2024 general election confirm FPTP's traditional strengths?

The Telegraph and *The Guardian* rarely find themselves in agreement, yet the initial sentiment that greeted FPTP's translation of votes to seats in 2024 was universally negative. *The Telegraph* denounced the electoral system as delivering a result that was 'the most distorted in UK history', while *The Guardian* declared that 'the UK's electoral system is creaking'. For many though, the 2024 general election merely provided another example of what the FPTP system does best.

Strength #1: first-past-the-post is easy to understand and outcomes are delivered quickly

First-past-the-post is among the simplest of all electoral systems in operation, needing no complex formulas or quotas to calculate the winner. The candidate with the most votes in each constituency is returned as the representative Member of Parliament (MP) and the government is formed by the party with the most MPs in Westminster.

- In 2024, within 24 hours of ballots closing, former Prime Minister Rishi Sunak had resigned and Labour leader Sir Keir Starmer had been invited to form a government by King Charles III. Within 48 hours of ballots closing, the new prime minister had appointed all his Cabinet ministers and had filled most government positions.
- The price to be paid for such a rapid, peaceful and efficient transfer of power from one majority government to the next is the way in which votes are translated into seats.

Strength #2: first-past-the-post delivers decisive results and stable governments

Majoritarian electoral systems are not intended to deliver results that accurately reflect the way that votes are cast. Indeed, the last time that a UK government secured more than 50% of the national vote was nearly a century ago in 1936. Majoritarian systems are instead designed to deliver quick results and stable, single-party governments. Aside from 2010, the use of FPTP has resulted in the formation of single-party governments following every general election since the Second World War.

- Despite the relative decline in Labour support, the outcome of the 2024 general election was another strong, single-party government able to enact its manifesto commitments unencumbered by lengthy multiparty negotiations or compromises with coalition partners.
- Although Labour received just over 9.7m votes, more than half a million votes down on 2019, their seat total rose by 211 to 412. The combined total of seats held by opposition parties, independent MPs and the Speaker was 246, giving the Labour Party a Commons majority of 158 seats.

Box 3.2 USA comparison

In the USA, FPTP is used in the election of members of Congress, including the House of Representatives and Senate, as well as for state legislatures and many local elections. In the presidential race, while the Electoral College ultimately decides the winner, each state (except

Maine and Nebraska) awards all its electoral votes to the candidate who wins the most votes in that state, following the FPTP principle. This approach often leads to clear, decisive outcomes but can also mean that a candidate wins the presidency without a majority of the popular vote, as was the case in recent elections.

In 2016, Donald Trump won the presidency with 304 electoral votes, while Hillary Clinton received 227. However, Hillary Clinton won nearly 2.9 million more votes than Trump, with Clinton securing around 48.2% and Trump 46.1%. Despite losing the popular vote, Trump won key swing states with narrow margins, which allowed him to secure a decisive victory in the Electoral College.

Box 3.3 Global comparisons

Some countries with more proportional electoral systems take many months to agree terms and form coalition governments. Recent examples include:

- **Israel** employs a pure proportional representation system, where parties win seats in the Knesset (parliament) based on their share of the national vote, provided they pass a 3.25% electoral threshold. This often results in fragmented parliaments with no single party gaining a majority, necessitating coalition governments. Following the April 2019 election, Israel faced political deadlock when no party could form a majority coalition. This led to an unprecedented series of repeated elections in September 2019, March 2020 and March 2021. It took about two years before a stable government was finally formed in June 2021, demonstrating how proportional systems can sometimes lead to prolonged negotiations and uncertainty.

- **Spain** uses a proportional representation system for its general elections, with seats in the Congress of Deputies allocated based on the D'Hondt method, a type of proportional representation. This system often results in a fragmented parliament where no single party gains an outright majority, necessitating coalition-building. After the general election in April 2019, no party achieved a clear majority, leading to a prolonged period of negotiations. The Spanish Socialist Workers' Party (PSOE) won the most seats but fell short of a majority, making it difficult to form a stable government. When coalition talks failed, another election was held in November 2019. Even then, forming a government took nearly two more months, resulting in Spain experiencing about ten months without a fully functioning government.

Strength #3: first-past-the-post leads to effective relationships between MPs and their constituencies, with clear accountability

FPTP's use of single-member constituencies provide two main strengths:

1. Unlike large, multi-member constituencies in which constituents can feel disconnected from their various representatives, single-member constituencies require MPs to represent *all* constituents and to reliably support the whole constituency.
2. The clarity provided by single-member constituencies means that it is relatively easy to hold MPs to account and vote them out of office.

One of the main strengths of FPTP is also the way in which it allows voters to pass emphatic judgements on the performance of a government. Under more proportional systems, governing responsibility can often be dodged as discredited and often unpopular parties continue to feature in coalition governments long after many voters have lost patience with them.

- 2024 saw FPTP maximising the size of the punishment inflicted on Rishi Sunak's Conservative Party leading to the worst electoral performance in the party's history. The decline in electoral popularity of the Tories saw their vote share collapse from 43.7% and 13.9 million votes in 2019, to 23.7% and 6.8 million votes in 2024. Although their national vote did not quite halve, the number of seats won fell to 121 – under a third of 2019's total of 365.

Is it time to replace first-past-the-post with a more proportional alternative?

The main arguments for replacing FPTP lie in the fact that it is both unfair and unrepresentative in the way that it translates votes to seats. 2024 was no different in this regard and saw a magnification of many of the distortions that occurred in 2019.

Weakness #1: first-past-the-post is fundamentally undemocratic

What is the democratic purpose of an election? If it is to create a representative assembly based on the voting preferences of an electorate then the 2024 election did not deliver on this. A large number of MPs in 2024 won their seats by slender margins – over 113 seats were secured with majorities of under 5%, many of which were won by Labour candidates.

Many MPs won seats with far less than 50% of the votes, as only a simple majority (one more than the nearest candidate) is required to win the seat. Three 2024 statistics stand out:

1. Labour received just over 9.7m votes, more than half a million votes down on 2019, yet their seat total rose by 211 to 412.

2. Labour's vote climbed just 1.6% in 2019 to 33.7%. In 2017 under Jeremy Corbyn, the party's vote share was 40.0% (262 seats).

3. Keir Starmer's own constituency support in Holborn and St Pancras fell more than 17% to 18,884.

Weakness #2: first-past-the-post marginalises 'minor' parties

One of the perceived strengths of FPTP is its preservation of a two-party system that allows for stable government and effective opposition. However, in 2024 the combined vote share for the two main parties was down to just 57.4%, yet the Labour and the Conservative parties still secured over 80% of the seats (535) between them. This was achieved by the continued marginalisation of minor parties.

- The Liberal Democrats ran a highly targeted campaign focusing mainly on seats where they were in second place to the Conservatives in 2019. It saw them secure 11.1% of the seats (72) from 12.2% of the national vote. While better represented than ever, the party is still under-rewarded.

- Reform UK came 'third' based on the 4.1 million votes they won. But despite taking 14.3% of the vote, the party secured just five seats, coming second in 98 seats. Reform's votes-to-seats ratio is greater than any disparity experienced by the Liberal Democrats.

- The Green Party won 1,841,888 votes but secured just four seats and has pledged to work to reform the electoral system.

For many, the increasing complexity of party politics in the UK looks set to see growing disparities between the rising support experienced by 'minor' parties and their inability to turn that support into seats.

Weakness #3 first-past-the-post discourages turnout and encourages tactical voting

One of the most concerning features of the 2024 general election is that turnout slumped to one of the lowest on record. In common with 2001 when turnout was similarly around 60%, all indicators had pointed to a sizeable Labour victory. It is difficult to establish who benefits most from a low turnout, but there is little doubt that FPTP, and the perception that votes can be 'wasted' in the many constituencies that appear to have a clear winner, can contribute to feelings of disillusionment among the electorate.

As well as disempowering voters, especially those living in 'safe' seats, critics of FPTP argue that any system which encourages voters to cast a vote for a candidate whose policies they may not agree with is flawed. Yet a YouGov study in late June 2024 indicated that while 22% of voters intended to use their vote tactically, Conservative voters were the least likely of the three main parties to do so.

Election year	Winning party	Size of majority	Turnout (%)
1992	Conservative	21	77.7
1997	Labour	179	71.4
2001	Labour	167	59.4
2005	Labour	66	61.4
2010	Conservative (coalition with Liberal Democrats)	No overall majority (coalition government)	65.1
2015	Conservative	12	66.1
2017	Conservative	No overall majority (confidence and supply with DUP)	68.8
2019	Conservative	80	67.3
2024	Labour	158	60.0

In England and Wales there is significant evidence that many Labour and Liberal Democrat voters were content to switch to support whichever of those two parties was best placed to defeat a Conservative candidate, thereby minimising the possibility of casting a 'wasted' vote.

For example, while Labour Party support across the country rose by less than 2%, in constituencies where Labour had previously come second their vote share rose by more than 6%. Additionally in those constituencies, despite a national rise in Liberal Democrat support, the Liberal Democrat vote share declined by around 1%. Conversely, where the Liberal Democrats were the leading challengers to the Conservatives in a constituency race, their vote share rose by over 9%, compared to under 1% nationally.

Additionally, while the UK-wide swing away from the Conservatives was 19.9%, their support fell by an even greater amount in seats that the Party was trying to defend. Reform UK's decision to stand candidates in all constituencies proved to be catastrophic for the Tories. Nationally, more than 4 million votes (14.3%) went to Reform UK and in 170 of the 244 seats that the Conservatives lost, such as Poole, the vote for Reform was larger than the margin of the Conservative defeat.

Chapter summary: do the weaknesses of first-past-the-post outweigh the strengths?

Factor	Yes	No
Did FPTP deliver a stable government?	Labour's landslide victory created a single-party government with a strong majority (158 seats), enabling decisive governance and clear opposition.	Recent examples, like the 2010 coalition and the 2017 minority government, demonstrate FPTP's occasional inability to deliver stable single-party rule.
Did FPTP provide fair representation?	Votes were rapidly translated into seats, allowing for quick government formation within 48 hours.	Disparities persisted: Labour won 63% of seats with just 33.8% of votes, while smaller parties like Reform UK (14.3% votes) secured only five seats.
Does FPTP encourage voter turnout?	Some voters may feel empowered in marginal constituencies, where their vote can directly influence results.	Turnout fell to 60%, one of the lowest on record, suggesting disillusionment with perceived 'wasted votes' in safe or uncompetitive seats.

Does FPTP strengthen two-party systems?	Labour and Conservatives held 80% of seats, preserving the traditional two-party dominance that provides stable government and opposition dynamics.	Minor parties like the Greens and Reform UK were heavily under-represented, reflecting limited space for alternative voices in Parliament.
Is FPTP simple and efficient?	Results are straightforward to understand and quickly calculated; the transition of power was peaceful and rapid.	Simplicity sacrifices proportionality, leading to significant distortions in how votes are translated into parliamentary representation.

Conclusion

The 2024 election outcome both exposed and magnified FPTP's strengths and flaws. While reforming the UK electoral system to a more proportional model could enhance representation, the failed 2011 referendum on the Alternative Vote shows limited public appetite for change. Additionally, there is little consensus on an alternative system, suggesting that significant electoral reform remains unlikely in the foreseeable future especially considering the unlikely possibility of a coalition of marginalised parties – including the Liberal Democrats, Reform UK and the Green Party.

Examination success

Sample essay examination questions:

- 'First-past-the-post should be replaced with a more proportional alternative.' Analyse and evaluate this statement. (AQA style, 25 marks)
- Evaluate the view that first-past-the-post should be replaced with a more proportional alternative. (Edexcel style, 30 marks)

Examiner's advice:

- When answering A-Level questions about whether the UK's first-past-the-post (FPTP) electoral system should be reformed in favour of a more representative system, students need to compare FPTP with alternative systems in use in the UK like the Single Transferable Vote

(STV) and the Additional Member System (AMS) as well as include examples of general election outcomes from before and after 1997.

- Most questions will require students to explain FPTP's several strengths, such as producing clear, decisive outcomes while highlighting several weaknesses, such as that stable governments can often be unrepresentative.

- Effective comparisons can be made with the outcomes of AMS for Scottish Parliament elections, which has produced more representative results, allowing smaller parties like the Scottish Green Party to gain seats, and the use of STV in Northern Ireland since 1998, which has helped to ensure representation across divided communities.

- However, the 2011 referendum on the Alternative Vote (AV) indicated limited public appetite for change.

CHAPTER 4
Voting behaviour in 2024: what factors explain Labour's victory?

What you need to know

- Historically, class has played a significant role in shaping UK voting behaviour, with working-class voters tending to support the Labour Party and middle/upper-class voters the Conservatives.

- In the UK, class-based voting was magnified by regional voting, with industrial north and inner-city voters disproportionately supporting Labour, and southern, rural and suburban voters supporting the Conservative Party.

- Dealignment refers to a decline in predictable (class-based or regional) voting patterns, while embourgeoisement is the process of working-class individuals adopting middle-class values and voting patterns, both leading to more volatile voting behaviours.

- Age, gender and ethnicity are all recognised as factors in shaping voting behaviour. For example, data indicates that a much higher proportion of younger voters vote Labour or Liberal Democrat while older voters tend to support the Conservatives.

- Recent decades have seen voters make more rational voting decisions based on how they believe parties will address key issues, rather than based on long-standing loyalty to a particular party.

- The appeal of party leaders, major events such as Brexit, the handling of the health pandemic, economic crises, party-political scandals, and the effectiveness of electoral campaigns can all influence voter behaviour in any given election.

- Explanations of voting behaviour in modern day elections have become more sophisticated, using terms such as 'positional' (the closeness of parties to the issues that matter most to voters) and 'valence' (consensus over which party or leader is more competent to govern).

Understanding the motivation of voters has been a preoccupation of academics and researchers for several millennia, indeed for as long as voting has existed. Psephology, the study of voting behaviour, takes its name from the Greek word psephos – the pebble that citizens dropped into an urn in ancient Athens to cast their vote.

Every election brings an opportunity to analyse similarities and differences in voting patterns, with the prevailing influences on voting behaviour in the UK changing over time. Where once whole voting blocs such as 'southern', 'young' or 'minority ethnic' could be reliably predicted to tend towards a certain party, dealignment – the steady separation of the once close relationship between class, region and party – has required the use of more refined voting models and theories to predict or explain election outcomes.

Box 4.1 Key definitions

- **Voting behaviour** refers to the way individuals cast their votes during elections, influenced by factors such as social class, age, ethnicity, region and political issues. It includes long-term factors, such as party loyalty and class alignment, as well as short-term factors, like the appeal of a party leader or specific policies. In the 2019 UK general election, Brexit significantly influenced voting behaviour. Many traditionally Labour-supporting constituencies in the north of England, known as the 'Red Wall', shifted to the Conservatives due to the Conservatives' clear stance to 'get Brexit done'.

- **Class-based voting** is the idea that individuals' social class determines their voting preferences, traditionally dividing voters into 'working-class' (Labour) and 'middle/upper-class' (Conservative). While this pattern has weakened in recent decades due to class dealignment, it still holds some relevance. Historically, the Labour Party's core support came from the working class, especially in industrial regions like South Wales and the north of England. However, the 2019 general election saw many working-class voters in these areas shift to the Conservatives, reflecting the declining influence of traditional class divisions in voting behaviour.

- **Voting models** are theoretical frameworks used to explain why people vote the way they do.
    - Sociological models focus on social group identity, such as class or religion.
    - Rational choice models suggest that voters make decisions based on a cost-benefit analysis of party policies.
    - Party identification models emphasise long-term loyalty to a political party.
    - Issue voting models highlight the importance of specific issues in determining voter choices.

2019 to 2024: similarities and differences

There are some key similarities in electoral outcome between 2019 and 2024:

- Both elections saw the creation of a stable, single-party government. In 2019, the Conservative Party won an 86-seat majority, while in 2024 the Labour Party won a total of 411 seats and an increase of 209 seats from the 2019 election.
- Both elections saw a high level of votes go to so-called 'minor' parties that were collectively under-rewarded in terms of seats won. In 2019, nearly a quarter of votes went to parties other than Labour or Conservative, yet those two parties won almost 90% of the seats. In 2024 this discrepancy was higher still: despite less than 60% of voters choosing Labour or Conservative, those two parties won well over 80% of the Commons seats.

Differences between 2019 and 2024 include:

- Voter turnout in 2024 was significantly lower at 60%, compared to 67.3% in 2019. 2024 marked the lowest turnout since 2001. Understanding the reasons behind, and impact of, non-voting is complex too.
- The impact of an 'insurgent' third-placed party was arguably the biggest single difference between the two elections. While the Brexit Party declined to stand candidates against incumbent Conservatives in 2019, Reform UK stood candidates in all constituencies. Reform won 4.1 million votes (14.3%), outperforming the Liberal Democrats by more than half a million votes but only won five seats compared to the Liberal Democrat's 72.

Box 4.2 Dealignment and realignment

- Dealignment occurs when voters no longer feel a strong loyalty to a particular political party. In 2024, data indicates that many 'traditional' Labour and Conservative supporters continued to focus on specific issues – such as immigration, investment in the NHS or perceived leadership qualities – rather than class-party loyalties thereby increasing voter volatility.

- Realignment happens when a disruptive shift occurs and voters develop a new long-term loyalty to a different party. In the 2024 election, the Green Party gained substantial support from younger voters, suggesting a potential realignment toward environmental issues influencing future voting patterns.

Does social class still play a major part in influencing voting behaviour?

The political forces unleashed by the 2016 Brexit referendum appeared to culminate in the 2019 general election outcome. Frustration and resentment over the lack of progress made to extract the UK from the EU, and Boris Johnson's personal appeal to new Conservative voters were key factors in shaping voting in the 2019 general election. By 2024, the Conservatives were perceived to have lost the trust of the average voter and the replacement of Jeremy Corbyn with Keir Starmer removed an obstacle to certain voters supporting Labour.

Three reasons why the **2019** vote indicated that class is less significant as a key determinant of voting behaviour:

1. The Conservatives were the most supported in all socio-economic groups by margins of between six points (among DEs – working class and non-working voters) and 20 points (C2 voters – skilled manual workers).
2. Labour's support fell further than average in constituencies with most voters in working class jobs – by an average of 11%. In 2019, the link between working-class voters and Leave voters was magnified by widespread disparagement for the direction that the Labour Party was perceived to have moved in.
3. The so-called breaching of the 'Red Wall' saw Leave-supporting seats in the Midlands and North, many of which had never returned a Conservative MP before, 'turned blue'. Former Labour Prime Minister Tony Blair's constituency seat of Sedgefield saw its 25,000 1997 majority turned into the Tory majority of 4,500 in 2019.

Three reasons why the **2024** vote saw a reversion to a more traditional class-party alignment:

1. The Conservative vote share among C2 voters (skilled manual workers) contracted significantly, dropping by 30 points from 52% in 2019 to just 22% in 2024. Reform UK capitalised on this, gaining 21% of the vote among C2 voters. While the Conservatives had more support from C2DE voters (working class) than ABC1 voters (middle class) in 2019, this reversed in 2024, with the party now having higher support among ABC1 voters.
2. The Conservatives saw a significant drop of 27 points among voters without degrees but only lost eight points among university-educated voters. Labour, on the other hand, gained 5% among non-degree holders but fell back by 4% among those with degrees, capturing 38% of this demographic.
3. Long-term realignment: Ipsos found that class differences between Labour and Conservative voters continued to narrow, with Reform UK performing best among C2 voters, reaching a vote share of 25%.

While there was a reassertion of class-party alignment in 2024, this could well be fleeting. Indeed, most studies of modern voting behaviour determine that class, age, gender and ethnicity have become less reliable predictors or explainers of voting behaviour due to the growing complexity and diversity of society. Voters are increasingly influenced by a range of factors, values and specific issues, rather than traditional identities. It has led to a more fluid and unpredictable electorate in recent years.

Positional theory and the Conservative collapse in 2024

The most significant explanation as to why large numbers of voters deserted the Conservative Party in 2024 lies in positional theory – the closeness of parties to the issues that matter most to voters. Unlike in 2019, most political commentators in 2024 concluded that none of the parties were especially well aligned with the 'average' voter. Labour was seen by many as too socially liberal and pro-immigration and the Conservatives were seen as too right wing economically and too nationalist. Distance from the average voters helps to explain why no party performed particularly well, and why turnout was low.

Box 4.3 Voting theories relevant to the 2024 outcome

Positional theory: voters choose the party that aligns most closely with their own policy preferences. This can be based on specific issues, such as a 'hard' versus 'soft' Brexit, or on broader ideological views, like the extent to which the government should intervene in the economy. This theory emphasises the areas where voters have different opinions about what they want the government to do.

Valence theory: voters select the party they believe is the most competent to run the country. This could be influenced by the party's past performance in office, its unity or whether its leader appears capable. This theory focuses on the areas where voters generally agree on what they want the government to do.

Positional factors that help to explain the average voter's move away from the Conservatives leading to a collapse in their support include:

1. **The nationwide impact of Reform UK**. Formerly the Brexit Party, the 2019 decision not to stand candidates against incumbent Conservative MPs had allowed Boris Johnson's 'Get Brexit Done' slogan to hoover up voters focused on the issue of the UK's delayed departure from the EU. In contrast, Reform UK's all-constituency challenge in 2024 was supported by more than 4 million voters, many of whom no longer saw the Conservative Party as the answer to their frustrations and to the issues that mattered most.

2. **The changing importance of issues.** Eve-of-election polling by YouGov helps to explain why a large number of voters deserted the Conservative Party in 2024. In 2019, 'leaving the EU' was one of the most important factors according to 62% of voters. It was ahead of 'Health' (52%) and well ahead of all other issues. The ground had shifted by 2024 when the twin issues of 'Health' (52% again) and 'Economy' (51%) led 'Immigration' (38%) and were far ahead of all others. Data indicates that Labour was more closely aligned to 'average' voters than the Conservatives on the two issues that mattered most. And for voters preoccupied by 'immigration', many saw a viable alternative to the Conservatives in Reform UK.

3. **The moderation of the Labour Party**. Keir Starmer's 'centrist' stances on key issues aligned more closely with the 'average' voter than Jeremy Corbyn in 2019. While Corbyn championed nationalising major industries, Starmer took a softer approach, focusing on pragmatic investments in public services. Corbyn's leadership saw a push for radical economic policies, including higher taxes for the wealthy, whereas Starmer aimed for a more balanced fiscal policy. Starmer's support for NATO and a pro-EU stance, compared to Corbyn's ambiguity on Brexit, also reflects his moderate positioning. Labour's perceived moderation meant that they moved closer towards the 'average' voters of the large centre-left.

Valence theory and the relative rise of the Labour Party in 2024

Vote collapses and landslide victories are rarely explained by one theory alone. Along with positional shifts between voters and parties, valence theory helps to explain Labour's victory in the 2024 UK general election by focusing on the importance of issues, party competence and leadership. While factors such as age, class and income may help to predict or explain aspects of voting behaviour, as Table 4.1 indicates, they declined across the board for the Conservative Party.

Consequently, rather than alignment based on traditional or ideological alignment, voters were swayed by perceptions that Labour was more capable of handling key issues like the economy, healthcare and public services. Additionally, Keir Starmer's reputation for strong leadership, in contrast to his opponents, reassured voters seeking stability and effective governance.

Table 4.1 The decline in Conservative vote among all groups

Age/class/income group	% Voting Conservative in 2024	Change since 2019 (%)
18–24	10	-25
25–34	15	-27
35–44	18	-30
45–54	25	-25

55–64	32	-28
65 and over	40	-20
ABC1 (middle/upper class)	30	22
C2DE (working class)	22	-30
Low income (<£20k/year)	20	-28
Middle income (£20k–£40k/year)	28	-24
High income (Over £40k/year)	35	-18

Source: adapted from Focaldata

The valence factors that help to explain the average voter's move away from the Conservatives leading to a collapse in their support include:

1. **The Conservatives lost the trust of voters on the economy.** Several years of high-profile economic failures and disappointments eroded confidence in the Conservative Party's ability to manage the economy. Liz Truss's mini-budget in 2022, which proposed unfunded tax cuts, led to market turmoil, damaging the party's reputation for fiscal responsibility. The cost-of-living crisis, with soaring inflation and rising interest rates, intensified public dissatisfaction, as many felt the government failed to protect them. Additionally, the high tax burden, partly a consequence of COVID-19 spending, contradicted traditional Conservative low-tax promises.

2. **Labour's relative competence was pivotal.** As indicated in Table 5.2, just one in three voters considered Labour fit to govern. Indeed Labour's polling data on 'trust' and 'fitness to govern' would have been worrying in the extreme for any opposition party in other circumstances. But in a two-party contest, relative competence is crucial, and the Conservatives' collapse gave Labour the advantage. It is also harder for voters to judge opposition parties' competence, as they lack a governing record, relying instead on general impressions.

3. **There was sufficient consensus on Keir Starmer's 'fitness to govern'.** Compared to 2019, Labour had a leader, Keir Starmer, who appeared more prime ministerial, uniting his party and presenting a

moderate image. Specific polling data that directly compared the party leaders indicated that 45% of voters rated Starmer as 'trustworthy', compared to 30% for his Conservative opponent. Fifty-two per cent believed he had the best plan for managing inflation, against 28% for the Conservatives (Source data: Dr Apurav Bhatiya, University of Birmingham).

Table 4.2 Party competence ratings 2019 to 2024 compared

On four key metrics, the Labour Party reversed previous deficits.

		2019	2024	Change
Can be trusted on the economy	Conservative	44	22	-22
	Labour	26	29	+3
Fit to govern	Conservative	46	15	-31
	Labour	29	31	+2
Best prime minister	Conservative	49	27	-22
	Labour	30	44	+14
Understands problems facing Britain	Conservative	46	20	-26
	Labour	47	39	+8

Source Ipsos, MORI, YouGov, 2024

Box 4.4 Comparison: proportional electoral systems and indecisive outcomes

In both the UK 2024 and US 2024 elections, economic concerns were pivotal, with voters reacting to issues like inflation and cost-of-living crises. In the UK and the USA, victory was influenced by dissatisfaction with the respective administrations of Rishi Sunak and Joe Biden and data indicated that victory for respective administrations of Rishi Sunak and Joe Biden. In the USA, data indicates that many swing-state voters trusted Donald Trump more than Democrat presidential candidate Kamala Harris to manage the economy.'

Differences include the polarisation levels: US elections were deeply divided along party lines, especially on issues like race, abortion and immigration, while the UK electorate focused more on competence and leadership. Additionally, the US saw historically higher turnout at well over 60%, while UK turnout was historically low, reflecting differing engagement levels.

Chapter summary: what factors explain the voting behaviour that determined the outcome of the 2024 general election?

Factor	Explanation	Evidence/example
Class realignment	A reversion to more traditional class-party alignment emerged, with working-class voters increasingly abandoning the Conservatives, wwhile Labour regained support among these groups.	Conservative support among C2DE voters dropped from 52% in 2019 to 22% in 2024, while Labour made modest gains. Reform UK also gained working-class support, especially among C2 voters.
Age and education	Younger and less-educated voters supported Labour and the Greens, while older, wealthier voters remained more Conservative, though with reduced enthusiasm.	Conservative support among 18–24-year-olds fell by 25 percentage points, and by 30 points among non-degree holders. Labour gained only slightly among non-degree holders but saw losses among degree holders, capturing 38% of this demographic.
Positional theory	Labour's centrist policies, under Keir Starmer, were closer to average voter preferences, while the Conservatives were seen as too right-wing economically. Reform UK captured disillusioned voters focused on immigration.	Starmer's moderate policies, such as pragmatic public service investments, contrasted with the Conservatives' economic policies, leading to Labour alignment on key issues like health (52%) and the economy (51%), while Reform UK gained 14.3% of the vote.

Valence theory	Voters perceived Labour as relatively more competent on key issues like the economy and healthcare, and Starmer as a trustworthy and capable leader.	Labour's competence ratings increased slightly, while Conservative competence fell sharply. Trust in Labour to handle inflation stood at 52% compared to 28% for the Conservatives.
Economic concerns	Discontent over the cost-of-living crisis, inflation and high tax burdens caused voters to lose faith in the Conservatives' economic management. Labour capitalised on this perception.	The Conservatives' reputation for fiscal responsibility was damaged by events like the 2022 mini-budget. Labour was perceived as better able to manage inflation, with 45% rating Starmer as trustworthy, compared to 30% for his Conservative opponent.
Turnout and third parties	Lower voter turnout and the rise of Reform UK disrupted traditional party dynamics. Reform UK siphoned off Conservative voters focused on immigration and dissatisfaction with the government.	Voter turnout was under 60%, the lowest since 2001. Reform UK won 14.3% of the vote (4.1 million votes) but only five seats, while the Liberal Democrats secured 72 seats with a smaller share of the vote.

Conclusion

Overall, the speed at which valence reputations can collapse provides a more effective explanation for the outcome of the 2024 general election. Just one in three voters supported the Labour Party – hardly indicative of a landslide victory – yet it was the plunging reputation of the Conservative Party, and therefore valence losses on qualities like economic competence, leadership and unity valued across the electorate that determined the result.

Examination success

Sample essay examination questions:

1. To what extent is class still the most significant indicator of voting behaviour in the UK? (Edexcel style, 30 marks)

2. 'Personalities rather than policies determine election outcomes in the UK.' Analyse and evaluate this statement (AQA style, 25 marks)

Examiner's advice:
Top-level essay responses on voting behaviour will include many aspects of the following:

- Analysis of how age, class, gender, ethnicity and region traditionally influenced voting patterns.

- Evaluation of the decline in traditional party loyalties, with examples of changing voting behaviour across age and class groups (dealignment and realignment).

- Explanations of how positional theories emphasising specific issues and the closeness of parties to average voters have come to the fore. In particular, how economic and social issues, such as employment, wages, the cost-of-living and immigration impact upon voter preferences.

- Evaluation of the role that classic valence issues such as competence, leadership and party unity shape voter decisions. Keir Starmer's leadership and the perceived incompetence of the Conservatives on economic matters heavily influenced the 2024 election.

- The extent to which media influence and the electoral campaigns affect voting behaviour.

- The best responses will use statistics and examples from recent elections (2019 and 2024) to demonstrate trends.

CHAPTER 5
The influence of mass media and artificial intelligence in the UK general election of 2024.

What you need to know

- The media significantly influenced voter perceptions and shaped key political narratives during the 2024 UK general election. Traditional outlets and digital platforms played key roles in framing party campaigns and setting the political agenda, impacting how the electorate viewed the candidates and policies.

- Traditional media, like TV and print, remain influential among older voters, while younger demographics engage more with new media platforms such as social media. These platforms not only spread campaign messages but also shape voter behaviour through grassroots movements and viral content.

- Media bias can manifest through framing, editorial choices and the selection of political stories. During the election, accusations of bias – whether intentional or unintentional – led to debates about impartiality. Persuasive techniques like emotional appeals were used to influence voter decisions.

- Artificial intelligence (AI) played a crucial role in the 2024 UK election, enabling micro-targeting, personalised messaging and even spreading misinformation. Tools like chatbots and predictive analytics influenced voter engagement, though they also raised concerns about electoral integrity.

- The UK election focused more on AI for micro-targeted messaging, while in the US, AI tools were used on a larger scale to shape voter perceptions and spread content. Comparing the two highlights differences in media and AI influence across political systems.

The mass media can be categorised into two broad terms:

1. **Traditional media**: This includes television, radio and print, which provide credibility and broad reach.
2. **Social media**: This encompasses platforms like X (formerly Twitter), Facebook, Instagram, TikTok and YouTube, enabling real-time interaction and dynamic communication between candidates and voters.

Different demographic groups use various media types to follow elections, raising concerns about social media, which is unregulated by Ofcom. Unlike newspapers, social media often lacks attribution, heightening the risk of disinformation being presented as fact.

This chapter will examine the role and impact of the media in the 2024 election, as well as the extent of media bias and persuasion.

Traditional media vs new media

A YouGov study conducted during the election showed that half of Britons followed the campaign closely, underscoring the media's vital role in shaping public engagement and awareness.

A significant majority of Britons relied on a single source for news: television, which accounts for 58%. Only 14% of the electorate still read printed newspapers, while a similar percentage (13%) is turning to podcasts. Although TV is the most commonly cited source, when all digital news formats are combined, 77% of Britons receive their news online in some form. In contrast, merging the 'broadcast' formats of TV and radio shows that 70% of Britons are getting their news through these mediums.

Table 5.1 How do Britons get their news?

Television	58%
Social media	43%
A newspaper's website or app	42%
Radio	42%
A news website or app not associated with a newspaper	33%
A printed copy of a newspaper	14%
Podcasts	13%
Emailed newsletters	7%
Blogs not associated with media organisations	4%
Other	3%

Which media is preferred by different party supporters?

Voters from Labour and the Liberal Democrats generally prefer to obtain their news from newspaper websites, with 47–51% relying on them, whereas only 37% of Reform UK supporters do so. Additionally, Labour and Liberal Democrat constituents are more inclined to gather news from non-newspaper websites (39–41%). Radio broadcasts are most effective for Liberal Democrat (49%) and Conservative voters (48%).

Labour and Liberal Democrat voters are also more likely to engage with podcasts for news (19%), while only 8–11% of Conservative and Reform UK voters do the same. Furthermore, Labour and Liberal Democrat supporters lead in accessing news through email newsletters (14%) and blogs not affiliated with major news organisations (11%).

Different demographics access politics via different media

Older individuals tend to rely on traditional news sources, particularly television, with 74% of those over 65 doing so compared to just 45% of 18–24-year-olds. In contrast, younger Britons are far more likely to acquire news from digital platforms, especially social media, with 72% of 18–24-year-olds engaging this way versus only 19% of those over 65. Overall, 90% of the youngest demographic consumes news online, while only 60% of the oldest do.

YouGov data (see Table 5.2) indicates that Facebook is the most widely used social media platform among British voters, with 69%. YouTube follows closely behind, utilised by 56% of voters, while Instagram is used by 46%. X (formerly Twitter) has a usage rate of 29%, and both LinkedIn and TikTok are used by 20% of voters.

	All Britons	Conservatives	Labour	Liberal Democrat	Reform	Green
Facebook	**69**	68	71	74	67	63
YouTube	**56**	42	62	60	61	66
Instagram	**46**	31	54	54	33	59
X	**29**	21	39	34	29	34

LinkedIn	**20**	16	25	25	14	26
TikTok	**20**	8	24	18	18	29
Reddit	**16**	7	24	20	10	26
Snapchat	**12**	5	13	12	9	17

Social media usage varies significantly across age demographics (see Table 5.3). For the three older age groups, Facebook remains the most popular platform, with usage rates between 69% and 72%. However, among 18–24-year-olds, Facebook drops to joint fourth place at 55%, sharing that position with TikTok. In this younger age group, YouTube and Instagram are the leaders, with 81% and 78% usage, respectively. Additionally, 60% of 18–24-year-olds are using Snapchat, while 50% engage with X (formerly Twitter).

Table 5.3 Which social media networks have different age groups used over the election period.

	18–24	25–49	50–64	65+
Facebook	55	71	72	69
YouTube	81	64	51	38
Instagram	78	60	34	18
X	50	35	27	14
LinkedIn	28	26	19	6
TikTok	55	25	12	4
Reddit	43	23	6	2
Snapchat	26	11	4	1

How many people have seen election-related content on social media?

Users of X and TikTok were the most likely to have encountered election-related content, with 60% of X users and 52% of TikTok users reporting that they have seen such content in the past 30 days (see Table 5.4).

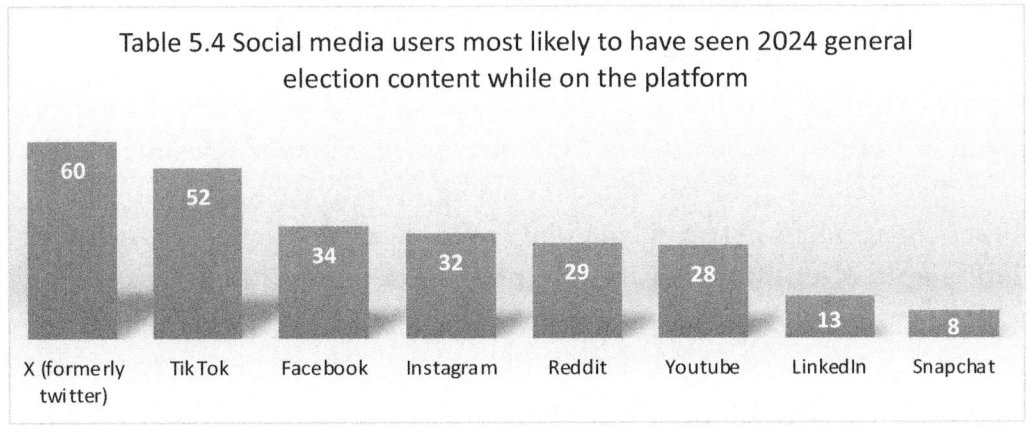

Table 5.4 Social media users most likely to have seen 2024 general election content while on the platform

Platform	Value
X (formerly twitter)	60
TikTok	52
Facebook	34
Instagram	32
Reddit	29
Youtube	28
LinkedIn	13
Snapchat	8

However, many of these platforms are only used by a minority of Britons.

- If we display these figures as a proportion of the entire population, as opposed to just the user base, we can see that:
    o The most common way people have encountered election content is on **Facebook**, at **23%**.
    o **X** still comes second overall, with **17%** of all Britons having seen election content on the platform.
    o Similar numbers have consumed it on **YouTube (16%)** and Instagram (15%).
    o One in ten Britons **(10%)** have watched election content on **TikTok**.

There are dramatic differences between age groups, however.

- Among **18–24-year-olds**:
    o More than four in ten **(44%)** have seen election content on **Instagram** in the last 30 days, making it the best platform for that group.
    o Another **36%** have seen **TikTok** election content.
    o A third **(33%)** have seen it on **YouTube**.
    o Another **30%** encountered it on **X**.

- By contrast, for older age groups:
    o **Facebook** is the most common way political content has reached people, at noticeably lower rates:
        ▪ **25–27%** of those aged between **25 and 64**.
        ▪ Only **19%** of the **over-65s**.

How important was the media in the 2024 general election?
The continuing importance of traditional media

Political campaigning has evolved significantly, yet traditional media remains a crucial component of the electoral landscape. Despite the rise of social media platforms, the essence of effective campaigning lies in direct engagement between candidates and their target voters. This direct dialogue is often hindered by the inherent delays in traditional media, where responses to published content take time.

- o However, traditional media still holds substantial power, particularly for the two main parties, Conservative and Labour, which dominate coverage.
- o Research from the University of Loughborough indicates that the Conservative and Labour parties accounted for 66% of appearances on main television news bulletins and 85% in the national weekly press, reinforcing their influence and limiting exposure for smaller parties.

The dominance of major parties in traditional media allows them to effectively set the political agenda and shape public discourse. The ability to control the narrative around key topics gives these parties a distinct advantage in the electoral process, effectively overshadowing smaller parties that struggle to gain similar media traction.

While digital media has transformed the way campaigns are conducted, traditional media continues to drive significant portions of political conversation.

- o Major legacy media outlets, such as newspapers and broadcasters, still command vast audiences, reaching over 20 million people in the UK each for publications like *The Sun, Daily Mail, Mirror, The Daily Telegraph, The Times* and *The Guardian*.
- o The BBC has an even larger audience, with 37.8 million users accessing its apps and websites alone.

This enduring influence underscores the fact that, despite the growing popularity of social media for news consumption, many voters are still relying on traditional media for information.

Traditional and new media: a symbiotic relationship

Moreover, the relationship between digital platforms and legacy media is often symbiotic. Many users on social media actively seek out content from established news organisations, following journalists and media brands to curate their newsfeeds.

- o 75% of online legacy news content is accessed through side-door routes such as social media, search engines and mobile aggregators.
- o This highlights the continued relevance of traditional journalism, as influencers on social media frequently draw from professional reporting to inform their commentary.

Politicians are acutely aware of the importance of traditional media and its ability to influence public opinion. The fact that leading politicians closely monitor the editorial preferences of major news organisations illustrates their recognition of traditional media's agenda-setting power.

- o For example, while a candidate may promote policies through social media, they often prioritise the potential reactions from influential newspapers over their online strategies.
- o This reflects a strategic understanding that traditional media can significantly impact voter perceptions and, ultimately, electoral success.

Box 5.1 Overview of social media strategies in the 2024 general election

Conservatives

The Conservative Party entered the 2024 general election with a robust social media strategy, supported by a considerable budget for high-quality content creation. Their tactics included:

- **High-quality production:** For instance, they released polished campaign videos that showcased key policies and candidate profiles, enhancing their professional image.
- **Analytical targeting:** They employed data analytics to deliver tailored advertisements to voters in swing districts, ensuring their messages reached the appropriate audiences.

Despite these advantages, the Conservatives struggled to convince voters that as the government that had preceded over the cost-of-living crisis, the immigration crisis and the NHS backlog they were the party to remedy these problems.

Labour

Labour effectively leveraged their grassroots campaigning philosophy across various social media platforms:

- **Live coverage:** They streamed rallies and community events on platforms like Facebook and X, fostering real-time engagement with potential voters.
- **Diverse content:** By combining professionally produced videos with spontaneous clips captured on smartphones, they appealed to a broad audience.

However, Labour faced challenges, such as:

- **Message inconsistency:** Confusion arose over key policies, like their stance on Corporation Tax, leading to mixed messaging that perplexed voters.

Smaller parties

Smaller parties also utilised social media with a significant degree of success:

- **Liberal Democrats:** They concentrated their efforts in critical constituencies, effectively using targeted ads to support local candidates in areas where they were competitive, such as in close races against Conservatives. The Liberal Democrat leader embarked on a series of bizarre publicity activities including bungee jumps to get his message across.
- **Reform Party:** This party successfully engaged younger voters through platforms like TikTok and Instagram, using relatable content and influencers to attract support from disenchanted Conservative voters. Nigel Farage's TikTok account generated the highest-performing content of the election campaign surpassing Labour's engagement by 30% and the Tories' by over twice as much between 22 May and 17 June.

Given the difficulty in breaching the dominance of the main parties in the traditional media, both parties deserved credit for getting their message across. The two smaller parties polled a combined 26.5% of the vote, nearly 3% more than the Conservatives.

Media bias, AI and persuasion

UK broadcast television and radio must adhere to strict standards of impartiality in news reporting. In contrast, print journalism is not obligated to maintain 'due impartiality' and may reflect political affiliations; however, the content is still attributable to journalists and must be based on credible sources. Social media stories, on the other hand, often lack attribution, contributing to the spread of 'fake news' without any evidential support.

All political parties face the challenge of combatting misinformation and disinformation on social media, making the rise of false information a significant concern. The potential for social media content manipulation by hackers, combined with AI-generated images and text, prompted platforms like Meta (the parent company of Facebook and Instagram) to introduce mandatory labelling for AI-generated images in February 2024. Numerous deepfake videos featuring prominent candidates surfaced, and while Luke Tryl, director of the More in Common think tank, expressed being "mortified" after being misled by viral clips of party members playing Minecraft with AI-generated voices, he was largely an exception.

Ahead of the July elections, AI experts cautioned Westminster to brace for a wave of misleading online content, particularly following disruptive events in Indian and Slovakian elections. Despite these concerns, the anticipated surge of AI-generated misinformation did not occur during the summer campaign, although there was considerably more controversy in the 2024 presidential election (see Box 5.2). Ales Cap, a researcher on deepfakes and elections at University College London, remarked, "The consensus seems to be that this [the UK 2024 general election] was a dull election. Everyone appeared to know the likely outcome. Malicious foreign actors likely had little interest in amplifying disruptive narratives."

Box 5.2 How disinformation defined the 2024 US presidential election

In the 2024 US presidential election, disinformation played a pivotal role in shaping narratives and influencing voter perceptions, particularly against President Joe Biden and Vice President Kamala Harris. There were also conspiracy theories online that the Trump assassination attempt had been faked.

Disinformation campaigns proliferated, disseminating outrageous claims such as:

- Immigrants were allegedly consuming pets.
- False stories about funding for undocumented immigrants during hurricane relief.
- A Russian-made hoax involved a fabricated video of a man falsely claiming to be Haitian and admitting to voting illegally in Georgia.

These narratives gained traction on social media, where memes and sensationalised content often overshadowed factual reporting. This environment, characterised by low trust in traditional media, allowed falsehoods to flourish.

As Elaine Kamarck and the author of *Lies That Kill: A Citizen's Guide to Disinformation* argued, the organised efforts to shape public opinion were systematic and extensive. Conversely, Elon Musk argued that X was a safe space for free speech.

Chapter summary: has social media become more important than traditional media in influencing election outcomes?

Factor	Yes	No
Social media's importance in influencing elections	Played a significant role in engaging younger voters through dynamic platforms like TikTok and Instagram.	Traditional media still dominant among older demographics and influential for setting the political agenda.
AI's role in election campaigns	Enabled micro-targeting, personalised messaging and efficient engagement through tools like chatbots.	Concerns over AI-generated misinformation did not materialise significantly in the 2024 UK general election.
Media bias and impartiality	Social media amplified disinformation and lacked regulatory oversight, unlike traditional broadcast media.	UK traditional broadcast media adhered to impartiality standards, maintaining credibility.

Traditional media's ongoing influence	Major outlets like the BBC and print newspapers continue to shape narratives for a large audience.	Limited reach and effectiveness among younger demographic who prefer digital platforms for news.
Smaller parties' use of media	Leveraged social media effectively to reach niche audiences and challenge the dominance of main parties.	Struggled to secure equal coverage on traditional media platforms dominated by Labour and Conservative narratives.

Conclusion

Despite the extensive media campaigns launched by the UK's political parties during the 2024 general election, the dismal turnout of just 52% indicated a collective failure to engage and persuade the electorate. Labour's landslide victory owed as much to the FPTP electoral system as it did to any mass enthusiasm on behalf of the electorate, as they were able win their 411 seats with just 33.8% of the vote.

This low level of participation suggests that traditional and digital strategies alike were insufficient in resonating with voters, leaving many feeling disconnected from the political process. The inability to mobilise support across diverse demographics reveals deeper issues regarding voter trust and engagement, highlighting a critical need for political parties to rethink their approaches and genuinely address the concerns of the electorate.

Examination success

Examination-style questions:

- 'Social media is now more important than traditional media in UK general elections.' Analyse and evaluate this statement. (25 marks, AQA style)
- Evaluate the view the view that newspapers are now having less of an impact in a general election than television and social media. (30 marks, Edexcel style)

Examiner's advice:

- Discuss how social media platforms influence voter behaviour by spreading information, shaping perceptions and by mobilising political engagement. Provide specific examples of campaigns where social media has played a decisive role, such as viral hashtag movements or targeted advertising.

- Examine the role of traditional media (e.g. newspapers, television) in influencing voter decisions, and compare this with the growing dominance of social media. Analyse how different demographics engage with both forms of media and which one has greater influence on voter turnout or voting patterns.

- Explore the extent to which media bias – either through selective reporting, framing or editorial content – affects voter perceptions and electoral results. Provide evidence of how biased coverage from traditional or social media has influenced specific election outcomes.

- Consider how AI algorithms are used to personalise political content, target voters and influence voting behaviour. Discuss the advantages and concerns surrounding AI in electoral campaigns, such as its ability to micro-target specific demographics or its potential to spread misinformation.

CHAPTER 6
The Constitution
The UK's constitution in 2025:
how is it changing under Labour?

What you need to know:

- The UK constitution is uncodified, consisting of statutes, common law, conventions and authoritative texts. Students should be familiar with its flexible nature, how it operates based on long-standing traditions, and how it differs from codified constitutions. Key areas to focus on include the separation of powers, parliamentary sovereignty, the role of the monarchy and the influence of European Union law pre-Brexit.

- Recent constitutional reforms include the introduction and elimination of fixed-term parliaments, devolution in Scotland, Wales and Northern Ireland, as well as discussions around House of Lords reform. Students must analyse both the successes and limitations of these changes in terms of improving democratic accountability and addressing regional imbalances.

- More recent constitutional reforms like the removal of hereditary peers, Labour's push for stronger local government powers, and ethical oversight mechanisms are crucial for evaluation. Labour's 2022 proposals aim to address regional inequalities, enhance democratic engagement and restore trust in politics. This includes more substantial devolution, greater local empowerment, and ethics reforms. Students should assess these plans' potential to transform UK politics.

- Labour's vision for the 'Assembly of Nations and Regions', the Council of the Nations and Regions for intergovernmental cooperation, and the rebalancing of power between Westminster and the devolved nations need to be evaluated. Students needs to consider their feasibility, political opposition and the potential long-term impact.

Box 6.1 Key definitions

- **Constitutional reforms** are changes made to the UK's constitutional arrangements, often aimed at improving governance, decentralisation or democratic accountability. Most recent constitutional changes took place under the Blair government in the years immediately after New Labour's 1997 landslide victory.

- **The Brown *Commission on the UK's Future (2022)*** was a comprehensive review led by former prime minister Gordon Brown on the future of the UK's constitution, culminating in a final report: '*A New Britain: Renewing our Democracy and Rebuilding our Economy*' focusing on regional devolution, economic fairness, and restoring public trust in politics. The report was largely adopted by the current Labour government and is currently being implemented.

Evaluating Labour's plans to reform the UK's constitution and progress made

The Labour government is in the early stages of reshaping the UK's constitutional framework through a set of transformative proposals outlined in Gordon Brown's 2022 *Commission on the UK's Future*. These constitutional reforms seek to address the UK's economic, democratic and trust deficits, with a vision for the most significant transfer of power from Westminster in modern history. Key areas include constitutional principles, devolution, intergovernmental cooperation, ethics and House of Lords reform.

Here we analyse the main principles of the Commission's final report and evaluate what has been done since Labour's 2024 general election victory to begin to achieve them.

Constitutional principles

The Labour government are aiming for a constitutional settlement to define the UK's purpose, especially emphasising the decentralisation of power from Westminster, the protection of social rights, and economic equity across the UK. The framework includes:

- **Decentralisation** in the form of legally mandating localised decision-making.
- **Social rights**, such as legally protected access to healthcare, education, housing and welfare.
- **Economic rebalancing** by guaranteeing equitable investment across regions.

While legally feasible, these principles require strong political and public support. Social rights, in particular, could expose government policy to judicial challenges.

Box 6.2 Case study: Labour's plan to rebalance the regions

Labour's Chancellor of the Exchequer, Rachel Reeves, unveiled plans to strengthen the role of regional mayors in boosting economic growth during the Great Northern Conference in Hull in 2024. This initiative targets economic disparities between London and the rest of England, where London's share of the national economy has risen to 24% since 2000, while other regions stagnate.

Reeves announced forthcoming policy documents on English devolution, emphasising strategic partnerships between mayor-led regions and the Department for Business and Trade. These partnerships aim to foster innovation and unlock regional potential by collaborating with businesses and universities. Additionally, Britain's innovation and research authorities will work with mayors to design long-term investment strategies.

Labour's broader economic vision seeks equitable growth across the country, addressing regional imbalances more effectively than comparable EU nations like Germany and France. This initiative aligns with Prime Minister Keir Starmer's mission to create 'good jobs and productivity growth' nationwide.

Source: adapted from Reuters, December 4, 2024

Devolution within England

Labour's plan prioritises devolving power within England to address regional disparities. Key proposals include:

- **Strengthened local governance** by expanding powers for mayoral combined authorities and encouraging regional partnerships without mandating mayors.
- **Community-level empowerment** by introducing police hubs and enabling communities to purchase local social assets.
- **Economic decentralisation** by relocating 50,000 civil service roles and allowing local governments to propose 'Special Local Legislation'.

Despite its ambition, implementation may face challenges such as slow timelines and potential dispute where powers potentially overlap between national, regional and local bodies.

Box 6.3 Case study: Civil Service People Plan 2024–2027

The UK government's Civil Service People Plan 2024–2027 outlines a comprehensive strategy to enhance the efficiency, capability and inclusivity of the civil service. Key initiatives include decentralisation efforts to advance the 'Places for Growth' programme by relocating 22,000 roles out of London by 2027 (with over 16,000 relocations achieved up to the end of 2024) to decentralise policy-making and leadership.

For more details see the **Civil Service People Plan 2024–2027**

Devolution to Scotland, Wales and Northern Ireland

The proposals offer modest new powers while reinforcing constitutional stability. Highlights include:

- **Safeguards for devolved powers** with a reformed second chamber charged with protecting them.
- **New powers** such as enabling Scotland to sign international agreements in devolved areas.
- **Enhanced privileges** through the strengthening of parliamentary roles for devolved legislatures.

However, contentious issues like independence referendums and Northern Ireland's political impasse remain unaddressed, reflecting Labour's cautious approach.

Box 6.4 Case study: Angela Rayner's 'Devolution Revolution'

At the September 2024 Labour Party Conference, Deputy Prime Minister Angela Rayner unveiled plans for a 'devolution revolution', pledging to decentralise power from Whitehall to local and regional leaders across the UK. Building on Labour's legacy of creating devolved institutions, Rayner emphasised enhancing powers for northern English mayors in areas like housing, transport and skills. Examples included successful Labour mayoral initiatives such as public transport reforms in Greater Manchester and West Yorkshire, showcasing the potential for locally driven change.

Rayner also announced a forthcoming white paper to outline Labour's vision for redistributing power nationwide. However, her speech indicated limited extension of these reforms to Scotland. Scottish Labour leaders expressed mixed views on further devolution, with opposition to proposals like a Scottish visa system.

Intergovernmental cooperation

To improve collaboration among UK governments, Labour proposes:

- **Solidarity clause** which sets out and mandates the need for cooperation across governments.
- The establishment of a '**Council of the Nations and Regions**' – a formal structure for regular leader meetings.
- **English regional representation**, including English regional leaders in intergovernmental discussions.

These measures aim to enhance inclusivity and address gaps in current frameworks.

Box 6.5 Case study: Labour's Council of the Nations and Regions

In 2024, the Labour government established the Council of the Nations and Regions to enhance coherence among the UK's governments. This body is made up of the Prime Minister, First Ministers of Scotland and Wales, Northern Ireland's First and Deputy First Ministers, and Combined Authority Mayors. Its primary objective is to facilitate collaboration on economic growth, public services and infrastructure development across the UK.

The inaugural meeting, chaired by Keir Starmer in October 2024 in Edinburgh, marked a significant step toward resetting intergovernmental relations. This initiative reflects Labour's commitment to decentralising power and promoting regional representation in national decision-making. The Council aims to address disparities and ensure that policies are attuned to the diverse needs of all UK regions. This approach seeks to strengthen the union by promoting mutual respect and cooperation among its constituent parts.

Ethics and standards

Restoring trust in politics is central to Labour's agenda. Proposed measures include:

- Transparency and increased oversight of political party donations and government transactions.
- Integrity oversight through the establishing of an independent Integrity and Ethics Commission to enforce a revised Ministerial Code.
- Citizens' juries to provide public oversight of political standards.

These reforms shift accountability from government to parliament while maintaining the prime minister's authority over ministerial sanctions.

Box 6.6 Case study: Labour's Ministerial Code and reforms to political standards

In November 2024, Keir Starmer introduced a long-awaited revised version of the Ministerial Code, aimed at setting clear standards for ministerial conduct. The updated Code, published after months of delay, incorporates changes such as restructuring the civil service into three parts, reintroducing compliance with international law, integrating the 'Nolan Principles', and giving more authority to the Independent Adviser on Ministerial Standards.

However, the Code has been criticised for being superficial and reactive, failing to address broader reform proposals, like establishing an Ethics and Integrity Commission. Key Labour manifesto commitments, such as legally enforceable post-government employment rules, have also yet to materialise. The resignation of Transport Secretary Louise Haigh shortly after highlights the continuing weaknesses in Labour's approach to ministerial accountability. This suggests a lack of progress in restoring public trust and reinforcing political ethics, leaving the government at risk of failing to deliver meaningful change.

Source: adapted from Mike Gordon's 'Labour's Ministerial Code and Political Standards Reform', U.K. Const. L. Blog (5 December 2024) (available at ukconstitutionallaw.org)

House of Lords reform

Labour seeks to eventually replace the House of Lords with an elected 'Assembly of Nations and Regions'. Key features include:

- Legislative oversight: scrutinising laws without control over taxation or spending.
- Constitutional safeguards: protecting statutes, with the Supreme Court clarifying powers.
- Proportional representation: possible use of elections to ensure fair regional and national representation to fill the second chamber.

While addressing criticisms of the unelected Lords, Labour must overcome historical obstacles to achieve this reform.

Box 6.7 Case study: New era for the UK House of Lords?

In October 2024, the UK House of Commons debated a bill introduced by the Labour government to remove the remaining hereditary peers from the House of Lords – a commitment made in their election manifesto. Hereditary peers, members of the nobility who inherit their titles and seats in the legislature, have been a longstanding feature of the UK Parliament. The reform is backed by Labour's significant parliamentary majority, alongside support from smaller parties, while the Conservative Party, representing the largest group of hereditary peers, opposes the bill.

The proposed change, expected to be enacted by mid-2025, would lead to a House of Lords comprised predominantly of life peers, alongside 26 Church of England bishops. The reform is seen as long overdue, addressing both legitimacy and gender imbalance issues, and is expected to enhance the chamber's ability to hold the government to account. This represents only the first step in broader discussions about further reforms, including limiting the chamber's size and improving the appointment process. Future debates may centre on transforming the House of Lords into an elected or part-elected body.

Source: adapted from Meg Russell, 'New Era for the UK House of Lords? Labour's Removal of the Hereditary Peers and Possible Future Reforms', ConstitutionNet.

Chapter summary of proposed constitutional reforms and steps taken

Proposal	What?	How?
Constitutional principles	Labour proposes a constitutional statement emphasising decentralisation, social rights and economic equity.	- Decentralisation: localised decision-making legally mandated. - Social rights: rights to healthcare, education, housing and welfare proposed to be embedded in law. - Economic rebalancing: Equitable regional investment guaranteed.
Devolution within England	Labour's plan focuses on devolving power to address regional disparities.	- Strengthened local governance through mayoral combined authorities. - Community-level empowerment: police hubs and community asset purchasing enabled. - Economic decentralisation: 50,000 civil service roles relocated.
Devolution to Scotland, Wales and Northern Ireland	Modest new powers with constitutional safeguards for devolved powers.	- Safeguards for devolved powers: Reformed second chamber for protection. - New powers: Scotland could sign international agreements; youth justice devolved to Wales.
Intergovernmental cooperation	Labour proposes mechanisms to improve collaboration among UK governments.	- Solidarity clause: mandating cross-government cooperation. - Council of the Nations and Regions: formal structure for regular leader meetings.

Ethics and standards	Restoring trust through increased transparency and an Independent Integrity and Ethics Commission.	- Transparency: increased oversight of government transactions. - Ministerial Code: revised version published.
House of Lords reform	Replace the House of Lords with an elected 'Assembly of Nations and Regions'.	- Removal of hereditary peers: bill introduced in 2024. - Legislative oversight: planned reforms to improve accountability. - Proportional representation: discussions on fair regional and national representation underway.

Conclusion

In 2022, Labour outlined ambitious constitutional reforms aimed at modernising the UK's political system. Since their election in 2024, the government has taken steps towards these goals, most notably by setting out clear plans to reset the relationship between regional and national governments, to empower local mayors and by introducing a bill to remove hereditary peers from the House of Lords. However, significant challenges remain. The reforms are still in the early stages, and much debate persists over further measures.

Examination success

Sample essay examination questions:
- 'Constitutional reforms in the UK should be taken further.' Analyse and evaluate this statement. (AQA-style, 25 marks)
- Evaluate the view that constitutional reforms in the UK have not gone far enough. (Edexcel-style, 30 marks)

Examiner's advice:
- Begin your answer by providing up-to-date examples of recent constitutional reforms, such as Labour's plans for devolution, ethics

reform, or House of Lords reform. This demonstrates clear knowledge and depth in addressing the topic.

- Analyse both the successes and the limitations of these reforms, such as Labour's decentralisation plans and their partial progress, providing evidence to support whether these reforms are comprehensive or merely symbolic changes.

- Explain how these reforms fit into the broader political, social and economic context in the UK. For instance, you could discuss how reforms like devolution address regional inequality but may not go far enough without financial devolution.

- Evaluate the immediate and potential long-term impact of these reforms, considering how reforms like the reformed House of Lords could lead to lasting institutional changes or be hindered by political resistance.

- A key area of evaluation is whether these reforms are likely to address the issues of democratic deficits, regional inequalities and trust in politics effectively or if they are more symbolic measures in the face of entrenched political structures.

CHAPTER 7
Has devolution worked and what next for the UK?

What you need to know

- Devolution refers to the transfer of powers and funding from national to local government. The most significant examples of devolution are the powers granted to the Scottish Parliament, the National Assembly for Wales, the Northern Ireland Assembly and to the Greater London and Local Authorities over 20 years ago.

- The original process of devolution formed part of New Labour's constitutional reforms back in 1997. Many saw these plans as seeking to neutralise nationalist sentiment, especially in Scotland and Wales, before they could grow into more dominant forces.

- Since then, the roles and powers of the devolved bodies have grown to become established parts of the UK's constitutional architecture. Yet alongside this development, nationalist causes and pro-independence movements within the territories have grown too.

- Scotland's independence movement over the last decade has been particularly turbulent. The 2014 #indyref saw the Scottish people vote narrowly (55:45) to remain in the union. Ten years later, YouGov polling indicates that pro-union sentiment remains at almost exactly the same level.

- Devolution and its future remain highly contested topics. Questions remain over whether a second Scottish independence referendum should be held; whether more power should be devolved to Wales; what the future holds for Northern Ireland; and whether England needs a national assembly.

In July 2024 there was a flurry of political activity relating to devolution in the United Kingdom. Within weeks of the Labour Party's general election landslide victory, Angela Rayner, deputy prime minister and communities secretary, had met with England's regional mayors in Downing Street and the King's speech opening the new parliament on 17 July 2024 had included the English Devolution Bill.

Mayors and local councils looked set to gain enhanced responsibilities for public transport, energy, infrastructure and skills; and policies for economic growth sought to tackle long-standing regional inequalities. In addition, a new body was set up to meet twice yearly. The Council of the Nations and Regions is made up of the leaders of Northern Ireland, Scotland and Wales, plus the metro mayors of England. The body's first meeting in October 2024 focused on a closer working relationship between the United Kingdom's constituent parts.

Box 7.1 Key definitions

- **Devolution** is the process by which central government in the UK delegates power to other levels of government. The Scottish Parliament, Welsh Assembly and Greater London Authority are examples of devolved institutions.
- **Metro Mayors** are directly elected by citizens in their area, and are chairs of their area's combined authority. In 2025 there were 12 metro mayors in the UK.

Devolution in 2025 – has it been a success?
The level of prioritisation by the newly installed Labour government indicated a renewed emphasis on devolution and regional power. However, nearly 30 years of devolution has met with limited success.

Yes, devolution has been effective
#1 Local policies are made closer to those affected by them. One of the key forces behind devolution was the aspiration to 'do things differently', allowing non-Westminster governance to pursue popular and relevant policies. In particular, local metro mayors are able to shape legislation, policies and priorities to better support and develop their communities:

- The Mayor of London's budget for 2024–25 included extending the Mayor's universal free school meals programme for all state primary school children for a further academic year until at least July 2025.
- In 2024, Greater Manchester mayor Andy Burnham sought a third term in office, with key pledges on improving housing and healthcare in the city.

One of the most significant recent developments has been the devolution deals to empower England's metro mayors who chair combined authorities, made up of constituent local authorities. From six in 2017, there are now 12 in post with further mayoral deals planned. In 2025, nearly half of England's population, accounting for more than half of its economic output, were overseen by a metro mayor. There is little doubt that greater local control over key areas like health, education and transport has allowed for policies tailored to local needs, reducing tensions over centralised control from Westminster.

#2 Regional legislation supports national distinctiveness. In the 25 years between 2000 and 2024 that the Scottish Parliament has been passing legislation, numerous acts have been passed, averaging 15 acts a year and peaking at 22 in 2016. Around 350 unique pieces of legislation have developed the region in distinctive ways and had a substantial impact on many aspects of life. Examples of recent acts include:

- *The Agriculture and Rural Communities (Scotland) Act 2024* which focuses on support for Scottish agricultural practices and the protection of animal welfare in Scotland.
- *The Visitor Levy (Scotland) Act 2024* which gave councils powers to introduce a visitor levy, sometimes known as a 'tourism tax', to generate funds to invest in local facilities and services.

The National Assembly for Wales has been able to pass primary legislation since 2008, averaging around five acts per year including recently:

- *The Environment (Air Quality and Soundscapes) (Wales) Act 2024* which made provisions for improving air quality in Wales.
- *The Infrastructure (Wales) Act 2024* which reformed the law governing the development of significant infrastructure in Wales and the Welsh marine area.

#3 The United Kingdom remains a functioning union of four nations. If one of the central planks of the devolution project was to preserve the union then, however strained relations may be, it has achieved this. This balance between unity and autonomy has strengthened the union by addressing demands for self-governance, promoting cooperation and mitigating nationalist pressures. As a result, devolution has proven vital in maintaining the cohesion of the United Kingdom.

Box 7.2 The nations of the United Kingdom work effectively together

The COVID-19 pandemic response

Despite sporadic hostility and deviation, throughout the COVID-19 pandemic the four nations (England, Scotland, Wales, and Northern Ireland) adopted a broadly coordinated approach to managing health crises. While each country had its own devolved powers, regular cross-border meetings between ministers helped align strategies, especially in areas like lockdowns, travel restrictions and vaccine rollouts, ensuring a consistent, albeit tailored, response to the virus.

COP26 Climate Summit in 2021

The UN Climate Change Conference (COP26) held in Glasgow brought together representatives from across the UK to present a unified stance on global climate action. This event demonstrated the success of devolution by allowing each nation to contribute their individual climate plans (Scotland's net-zero targets, Wales' renewable energy goals, Northern Ireland's climate strategies), while also working collaboratively with one voice towards international agreements on emissions reductions.

Cross-border trade and economic cooperation

In recent years, the four nations have cooperated closely on trade, particularly with regard to the Northern Ireland Protocol. This agreement, negotiated as part of Brexit, required the four governments to work together to ensure the smooth movement of goods between Northern Ireland and the rest of the UK, safeguarding cross-border trade while addressing EU regulations – showing that devolution has supported practical, unified economic approaches.

Support for refugee crises (Ukraine, Afghanistan)

The response to international refugee crises, like the ongoing situation in Ukraine and the evacuation efforts from Afghanistan in 2021, showcased cross-national solidarity. The UK nations came together to coordinate the welcoming, resettlement and humanitarian aid efforts, demonstrating their ability to unite when faced with global challenges, while still respecting devolved powers in areas like immigration and asylum.

No, devolution has not succeeded in its primary goals

Devolution in the UK was intended to bring greater autonomy to Scotland, Wales and Northern Ireland, granting these nations control over various aspects of their governance, such as health, education and justice, while maintaining a level of cooperation with the UK Parliament. However, since the early 2000s, devolution has faced several challenges that have undermined its success. The inability to deliver cohesive, fair governance across all four nations, combined with political instability, economic disparities and poor cross-border cooperation, has limited devolution's effectiveness.

#1 Economic inequality and disparities exist between nations

One of the key failures of devolution has been the persistent economic inequalities between the UK's constituent nations. Despite having devolved powers over areas like economic development, taxation and infrastructure, the economic growth in Scotland, Wales and Northern Ireland lags behind that of England. For example, in 2024, reports showed that Scotland's economic performance had weakened, with high unemployment rates in certain areas and slower recovery from the pandemic. The lack of consistent investment and varying economic strategies between the devolved administrations has meant that opportunities are unevenly distributed, failing to narrow the regional economic divide. Devolution was designed to address such imbalances, yet it has only deepened regional inequalities.

Box 7.3 Case study: Scotland's declining economic performance

Scotland's productivity has continued to lag behind the rest of the UK, according to the latest CBI-Fraser of Allander Scottish Productivity Index, published in March 2024. The report highlights that Scotland trails behind in ten of the 13 productivity indicators, including business investment, exports, skill shortages and economic inactivity. Long-term sickness remains the highest among the four UK nations at 37.1%, while business investment as a share of GDP contracted by 0.3% in 2022, underperforming the UK average.

Despite some recovery since the pandemic, improvements in business innovation and trade openness remain slow, falling below the UK average. Professor Mairi Spowage from the Fraser of Allander Institute emphasised that Scotland's productivity struggles are exacerbated by the dominance of London and the southeast of England. She highlighted the urgent need to address workforce health, noting a worsening in sickness absence and long-term inactivity, supported by the rising numbers claiming disability-related benefits. The National Strategy for Economic Transformation (NSET), which focuses on employability programmes, has faced setbacks due to budget cuts, limiting its impact.

Tracy Black, CBI Chief Strategy Officer, warned that Scottish firms need to focus on embracing innovation and technology to improve productivity. With a highly educated workforce, there is potential for economic growth, but this requires greater investment in leadership development and digital proficiency. Without these efforts, Scotland risks falling further behind.

Source: Adapted from the University of Strathclyde: 'Latest productivity index shows Scotland lagging behind the rest of the UK' (March 2024).

#2 A devolved UK is often characterised by political instability and lack of consensus

Another significant issue is the frequent political instability that has arisen due to differing priorities among the devolved governments. In recent years, particularly in 2024, this has been seen with tensions between Westminster and the devolved administrations. For example, in Northern Ireland, the power-sharing agreement between the Democratic Unionist Party (DUP) and Sinn Féin has repeatedly broken down. The Welsh government faced ongoing challenges in areas such as health care funding and infrastructure investment, which were compounded by disputes with the UK government over budget allocations and decision-making powers. For example, disagreements between the Welsh First Minister and the UK government regarding the allocation of financial resources for public services led to delays in key projects and strained relations. These recurring conflicts highlight the inability of devolution to deliver coherent and sustainable policy outcomes, as power struggles and competing interests hinder effective collaboration between Wales and the rest of the UK, leading to political deadlock and prolonged periods without functioning governance.

Box 7.4 Case study: Welsh disputes and disagreements

In 2024, tensions between Wales and the UK government came to the forefront with the resignation of Vaughan Gething, the Labour leader of Wales. Gething's brief tenure as first minister was marred by internal party conflict, accusations of misconduct, and his handling of donations from a controversial source, which led to a vote of no confidence. This deepened the divide between Cardiff and Westminster, reflecting ongoing struggles over power and governance.

The resignation highlighted the growing instability in Welsh politics, where tensions over key policy areas – such as health care and transportation – continue to clash with the priorities of the UK government. For example, the Welsh government's push to implement 20mph speed limits sparked debates over devolved powers, with critics in Westminster arguing it was an example of overreach. These disagreements underline the broader issue of balancing local autonomy with the wider interests of the UK, creating frequent clashes between Wales and the rest of the UK on decision-making, financial allocations and the scope of devolved powers.

Gething's departure provided an opportunity for Welsh Labour to reset, but it also exposed the deeper challenges facing devolution in Wales – namely, the struggle to maintain unity and deliver long-term improvements in areas like health care, while simultaneously managing relations with the UK government.

Source: Adapted from *The Guardian* 'Vaughan Gething's exit gives Welsh Labour a chance to reset' (July 2024).

#3 Effective cross-border cooperation has been challenging

A fundamental goal of devolution was to foster better cooperation across the four nations of the UK. However, in practice, this has not materialised effectively. Brexit in 2020 revealed significant weaknesses in cross-border collaboration, which exposed the limitations of devolution. For example, in 2024, tensions over the implementation of the Northern Ireland Protocol led to renewed disputes between the UK government and the devolved administration in Northern Ireland, with trade disruptions causing economic harm. Devolution was supposed to allow nations to work together on shared interests, yet such issues have proven difficult to navigate due to conflicting priorities and a lack of effective communication between administrations.

Box 7.5 Case study: Northern Ireland's instability

More than four years after the UK's departure from the EU, Northern Ireland continued to grapple with political instability, with a fragile peace still under strain. In January 2024, nearly two years of gridlock ended with the UK government presenting a new deal aimed at restoring power-sharing in Belfast. The plan promises to ease tensions by reducing trade checks between Britain and Northern Ireland, but it does little to address the deep-rooted divisions. The Democratic Unionist Party (DUP), which had boycotted government, agreed to return, but only after substantial pressure and compromises.

Despite some cautious optimism, the challenges are far from resolved. The DUP's leader, Jeffrey Donaldson, admitted that the deal was not perfect, conceding that compromises were made. The deal, known as the 'Safeguarding the Union', aimed to bolster Northern Ireland's position within the UK, but critics argue that it fails to address underlying economic issues and the ongoing tensions around Brexit, such as the invisible border in the Irish Sea.

As the fallout from Brexit continues, Northern Ireland's political and economic landscape remains fragile. The region's healthcare system is overstretched, public-sector workers face wage stagnation, and rising tensions threaten stability. This agreement, while a step forward, is merely a temporary reprieve, highlighting the difficult legacy Brexit has left on Northern Ireland.

Source: Adapted from *The New York Times* 'In Northern Ireland, a Knotty Brexit Problem Is on the Brink of Being Solved' (February 2024).

Comparison: devolution in the UK vs federalism in the USA

- Structure and authority: In the US, federalism is clearly divided between state and federal governments, with specific enumerated powers granted to both. The US Constitution explicitly outlines state versus federal responsibilities (e.g. taxation, healthcare). In contrast, devolution in the UK allows for powers to be transferred from the central government (Westminster) to devolved administrations (Scottish Parliament, Welsh Assembly), but it remains subject to parliamentary sovereignty, making it more flexible but less autonomous.

- Economic disparities: In the US, federalism often exacerbates economic inequality, as states have different levels of autonomy and access to resources. For example, states like California have stronger economic policies compared to others, like Mississippi. In contrast, devolution in the UK has had mixed success, as areas like Scotland and Wales face significant regional economic disparities despite devolved powers over areas such as health and education.

- Cross-border cooperation: In US federalism, cross-border cooperation can be limited due to political differences between state governments, with notable challenges in areas like healthcare reform and environmental regulation. Meanwhile, UK devolution has shown better cooperation, such as in shared strategies during events like the COVID-19 pandemic and COP26, though tensions still exist, particularly between Northern Ireland and Westminster.

What next for devolution in the UK?

Some commentators argue that devolution in the UK can be made a success by addressing key challenges and building on the existing framework through various strategies. One approach involves further decentralisation of powers.

- Currently, Scotland, Wales and Northern Ireland each have devolved governments with varying degrees of authority, but many argue that these powers do not extend far enough to meet the needs of local populations.

- The Scottish government has repeatedly called for increased control over areas such as taxation, welfare and economic policy to better align decisions with the priorities of the Scottish electorate. Expanding devolution in this way could empower local governments to implement policies that are more responsive to regional demands.

A second theory focuses on greater financial autonomy for the devolved administrations. Devolution has resulted in varying degrees of fiscal power, but in practice, these governments still rely heavily on funding from Westminster.

- The Barnett Formula, which allocates funding to Scotland, Wales and Northern Ireland, has been criticised for failing to accurately reflect population changes and economic needs.

- Increasing financial independence would allow the devolved governments to craft budgets that better address local priorities, such as investing in infrastructure, education and healthcare specific to their regions. This would create greater accountability and responsiveness to regional demands.

A moderate approach could be taken by introducing a more flexible system that allows for both shared decision-making and regional autonomy.

- Recent discussions around the 'Westminster Model' of devolution highlight the potential for more flexible cooperation between Westminster and devolved bodies. This model could ensure that key areas, such as trade, defence and foreign policy, remain under UK-wide control, while other areas, like health, education and transport, are devolved.

- A balanced approach would help maintain unity while enabling regions to tailor policies to their specific needs.

Chapter summary: devolution in the UK – has it worked and what next?

Factor	Success	Failure	What next?
Local policies made closer to communities	Local metro mayors are able to shape policies that address community-specific needs, like free school meals and housing improvements.	Economic inequalities between nations persist despite devolved powers. Scotland, Wales and Northern Ireland lag behind in economic growth.	Expand devolution to give more control over taxation, welfare and economic development to better align local governance with regional needs.
Regional distinctiveness in legislation	The Scottish Parliament and National Assembly for Wales have passed significant acts that reflect their regions' distinct priorities.	Varying degrees of success in legislation, with limited impact on addressing economic disparities and political instability.	Encourage more cross-border cooperation on shared legislation and funding decisions, while allowing tailored policies in health, education and transport.
United Kingdom remains cohesive	Devolution has helped maintain the union by addressing nationalist pressures through autonomy and cooperation.	Political instability persists, with ongoing disputes in Northern Ireland and Wales affecting governance and unity.	Foster more flexible devolution models that ensure national unity while allowing regional autonomy in key areas like trade, defence and infrastructure.

Conclusion

Devolution has not achieved its intended success. Economic disparities, political instability and poor cross-border cooperation continue to hinder the progress of devolution in the UK. Recent events, such as the ongoing Brexit-related challenges in 2024, exemplify the limitations of devolution, demonstrating that it has failed to deliver on its primary goal of providing effective and cohesive governance across all the UK nations.

Examination success

Examination-style questions:

- 'Devolution in the UK has not gone far enough.' Analyse and evaluate this statement. (25 marks, AQA style)
- Evaluate the view the view that devolution in the UK has been a success. (30 marks, Edexcel style)

Examiner's advice:

- Make sure you have a clear grasp of the main elements of devolution in the UK, including the powers and responsibilities granted to the devolved governments (in Scotland, Wales and Northern Ireland), as well as the ongoing debates about centralisation versus decentralisation.

- Incorporate recent and relevant examples from 2024 and beyond to support your analysis. Examples such as Brexit's impact on Northern Ireland, the fiscal challenges faced by devolved governments, or any specific policy disputes between Westminster and devolved administrations will strengthen your arguments.

- Organise your answer into clear, well-structured paragraphs. Start with an introduction that outlines your key points, followed by separate sections that critically analyse and evaluate devolution. Conclude by summarising your evaluation and providing a reasoned judgement.

- Address multiple viewpoints in your response. Consider the arguments for and against the success of devolution, such as the benefits of local decision-making versus the challenges of maintaining coherence and economic equality across the UK. This will show a balanced understanding and improve your evaluation.

CHAPTER 8
Parliament
The UK parliament in 2025: how well does it function?

What you need to know:

- The structure of the Commons and Lords: understand the composition, roles and functions of the elected House of Commons and unelected House of Lords.
- The powers of the Commons and Lords: analyse the Commons' supremacy in law-making and confidence votes versus the Lords' revising and delaying powers.
- The legislative process: study and evaluate the effectiveness of the stages of a bill, including readings, committee scrutiny, amendments and royal assent for law-making.
- Parliament-executive relationship: explore how Parliament scrutinises, limits and collaborates with the executive through debates, committees and votes of no confidence.

Box 8.1 Key definitions

- The **Salisbury Convention** in the House of Lords does not block legislation promised in the governing party's manifesto, respecting the democratic mandate of the House of Commons.
- The **Parliament Acts** of 1911 and 1949 limit the Lords' power, allowing the Commons to bypass them to pass legislation after only a short delay.
- **Hereditary peers** are individuals who inherit their titles and membership in the House of Lords, historically holding significant social and political influence.
- **Three-line whips** are strong party instructions for MPs to vote in a specific way, indicating that their attendance and compliance are crucial.

How effective is the House of Lords in 2025?

The UK House of Lords plays a prominent and valuable role in the legislative process by scrutinising bills, proposing amendments and holding the government accountable. Comprising experts from various fields, it enhances legislation through detailed analysis. While unelected, its effectiveness lies in using the considerable expertise and experience to refine laws, protect rights and ensure long-term considerations are addressed, thereby complementing the work of the elected House of Commons.

A complementary legislative role

The House of Lords plays a crucial role in supporting the elected House of Commons by scrutinising legislation and ensuring its detailed provisions are effective and achievable. Unlike the Commons, which is often driven by partisanship and re-election priorities, Lords attempt to take a longer-term view, focusing on refining bills and using their expertise and experience to improve the quality of UK legislation.

In 2024, the House of Lords sought to enhance the controversial Rwanda Asylum and Immigration Bill by proposing amendments that clarified the treatment of asylum seekers, mitigating potential legal challenges. This demonstrated its ability to refine complex legislation while respecting the Commons' primacy, as dictated by conventions like the Salisbury Convention. However, the Lords' effectiveness is limited by its inability to reject bills outright, even when substantial concerns are raised. Strengthening the legislative veto powers of a more legitimate second chamber could further improve Parliament's oversight functions without undermining democratic accountability.

Box 8.2 Case study: Lords' refinements rejected

In March 2024, the UK House of Commons rejected all ten amendments proposed by the House of Lords to the Safety of Rwanda (Asylum and Immigration) Bill, restoring it to its original form. This legislative move aimed to facilitate the deportation of asylum seekers to Rwanda, a central component of Prime Minister Rishi Sunak's strategy to deter dangerous Channel crossings and address illegal immigration.

The Lords had introduced amendments to ensure compliance with domestic and international law, assess Rwanda's safety as a destination, and protect individuals with specific vulnerabilities. Despite these concerns, the Conservative majority in the Commons voted down the amendments, underscoring the government's commitment to its original policy. This decision provided a significant boost to Prime Minister Sunak amid internal party challenges and declining poll ratings. The bill received Royal Assent on 25 April 2024, becoming law.

Expertise and legislative scrutiny

The Lords' composition is unique, with appointed members bringing expertise from diverse fields such as the armed forces, business, academia, law, medicine and public service. This qualitative merit allows for detailed examination of legislation, often neglected in the Commons, where MPs are often required to prioritise constituency work. The House of Lords secured over a thousand amendments to government bills in 2023–24. The Levelling-Up and Regeneration Bill in 2024 exemplified this expertise. Peers debated and deliberated extensively to address complex amendments, ensuring the legislation met its intended goals.

Box 8.3 Case study: legislative enhancement

The Levelling-Up and Regeneration Bill 2024 underwent significant review in the Lords, where peers proposed amendments to enhance its effectiveness. Concerns were raised about environmental protections, local governance powers and housing development regulations. Lords' debates led to changes that better balanced national goals with local needs, and address gaps to ensure clearer guidelines for sustainable development.

Independence and government accountability

The absence of a government majority in the Lords ensures a culture of justification, where ministers must persuade peers across party lines. This independence was evident in 2024 when the Lords resisted aspects of the Public Order Bill, raising concerns over potential overreach in policing protests. Such resistance highlights its value in holding the government to account and safeguarding civil liberties.

However, the Lords' ability to delay legislation is constrained by the Parliament Acts, limiting its power to effect substantial change. Expanding its powers to scrutinise statutory instruments – secondary legislation that often bypasses rigorous Commons debate – could bolster its role as a check on executive authority.

Box 8.4 Case study: scrutiny and expertise

The Public Order Bill 2024 was extensively reviewed by peers to ensure that its provisions balanced public safety with individual rights. During scrutiny, peers raised concerns about potential overreach in protest restrictions and the impact on civil liberties. Amendments were proposed to clarify the definitions of key terms and limit the scope of police powers. These changes ensured the bill upheld the rule of law while protecting fundamental freedoms. This highlights the Lords' crucial function in safeguarding rights and improving legislative clarity.

Agenda-setting and policy innovation

The Lords also plays a vital role in setting the legislative agenda and addressing issues overlooked by the Commons. Its select committees and debates bring attention to long-term challenges, such as climate change and public health. In 2024, peers raised awareness of post-pandemic mental health issues, prompting government action to allocate additional funding to NHS mental health services.

Despite these contributions, the Lords' influence is often overshadowed by public scepticism about its unelected status. Introducing partial elections, alongside appointed members with proven expertise, could enhance its legitimacy while preserving its independence and agenda-setting capacity.

Box 8.5 Case study: research and investigation

In 2024, the House of Lords played a key role in raising awareness of post-pandemic mental health challenges through committee activity. The Lords' Public Services Committee conducted a detailed inquiry into the mental health crisis exacerbated by COVID-19, highlighting critical gaps in NHS mental health services and the strain on young people and underserved communities. Their findings led to recommendations for urgent government intervention. In response, the government announced additional funding to expand mental health services, demonstrating the Lords' impact in spotlighting urgent social issues and prompting actionable change.

Box 8.6 What are the ways to reform the UK's second chamber?

The UK House of Lords has long been a subject of reform discussions, with recent proposals aiming to modernise its composition and function. Notable reform proposals include:

1. **Abolition of hereditary peers**: in 2024 the Labour government introduced the House of Lords (Hereditary Peers) Bill, seeking to remove the remaining hereditary peers from the House, thereby ending the practice of aristocratic succession in legislative roles.

2. **Establishing an elected second chamber**: the Brown Commission (2022) proposed replacing the House of Lords with an elected 'Assembly of the Nations and Regions', aiming to enhance democratic legitimacy and better represent the UK's diverse constituencies.

3. **Implementing a mandatory retirement age**: Labour plans to introduce a mandatory retirement age for peers, ensuring the infusion of new perspectives and addressing concerns about the ageing composition of the House.

These proposals reflect ongoing efforts to reform the UK's second chamber, balancing tradition with the need for a more representative and accountable legislative body.

Case study: fast-tracking reform

The Times, in September 2024, outlined plans to fast-track the removal of hereditary peers from the House of Lords within 18 months. The government's legislation to abolish all 92 hereditary seats, ending law-making by 'accident of birth', marked a significant step in reforming the UK's second chamber. Labour leaders highlighted the move as fulfilling a manifesto pledge and modernising the chamber. Proposals included compulsory retirement for peers over 80 as part of broader reforms.

Source: adapted from *The Times*, 'House of Lords reform to remove hereditary peers in 18 months,' 5 September 2024.

How well does the current UK Parliament perform its functions?

Any examination of the effectiveness of the UK Parliament's roles needs to consider the composition, structure and procedures of Parliament, all of which have an impact on MPs and their ability to represent constituents.

Implications of the 2024 election result

The 2024 UK general election significantly shaped Parliament's representative and legislative functions. Labour's decisive victory, securing a majority of 118 seats, underscored widespread public discontent with the Conservative Party's economic management and positioned Sir Keir Starmer as a prime minister capable of addressing voters' concerns. However, this large majority also presented challenges to Parliament's ability to represent diverse perspectives effectively.

A commanding government majority often leads to restricted debate and scrutiny in Parliament, as party discipline ensures that the ruling party's legislative agenda proceeds largely unconstrained. This was evident during the January 2025 amendment to the Children's Welfare Bill. The amendment, which imposed controversial caps on foster care allowances and much-publicised Conservative party amendments, faced limited resistance from Labour MPs despite widespread criticism. A three-line whip ensured that even dissenting MPs were forced to vote in favour, raising concerns about whether Parliament adequately reflects constituents' diverse views.

Weakness of the opposition

The aftermath of the 2024 election saw the opposition's role in representing alternative perspectives greatly diminished. The Conservative Party, reduced to 121 seats, struggled to challenge the government effectively, with its credibility undermined by a disastrous electoral performance. The Liberal Democrats and other smaller parties, though slightly increasing their seat counts, remained too fragmented to exert meaningful influence.

This imbalance weakened Parliament's ability to hold the government accountable and represent a broader spectrum of public opinion. For instance, debates on Labour's Green Housing Initiative in late 2024 saw limited scrutiny of its implementation costs and feasibility. A robust opposition could have amplified concerns from voters who felt the policy prioritised urban areas over rural communities. Parliament's functioning suffers when the opposition is too weak to reflect robustly the concerns of all constituents.

Box 8.7 Case study: the House of Lords as an effective opposition?

In periods of weak and diminished opposition in the Commons, the House of Lords can serve as a more effective counterbalance to a dominant government majority. In 2024, the Lords effectively challenged the government's controversial Public Health Bill, proposing significant amendments aimed at enhancing public health protections. Their ability to introduce informed debate and constructive criticism exemplifies how the Lords can fulfil a vital opposition role, ensuring that government actions are thoroughly examined and debated.

Weakness of individual MPs

Parliament's functions are further undermined by the declining influence of individual MPs. The dominance of party leaderships, reinforced by mechanisms like the three-line whip, curtails MPs' ability to act independently in representing their constituents' interests.

Careerism among MPs also affects their representative role. Many MPs, particularly those in marginal seats, focus on maintaining party favour to secure re-election or future ministerial roles. This has led to accusations of a Parliament that is increasingly populated by career politicians with limited expertise outside of politics, diminishing the diversity of perspectives needed for effective representation.

Box 8.8 Rishi Sunak: just one parliamentary defeat in two years

In December 2023, an amendment to the Victims and Prisoners Bill aimed at establishing a body to provide restitution for victims of the contaminated blood scandal came to a crucial vote. Despite the government imposing a three-line whip against the amendment, Home Affairs Select Committee Chair Dame Diana Johnson pushed for the vote, and Labour announced its support just a day prior. The amendment narrowly passed with a vote of 246–242.

The vote represents Rishi Sunak's only parliamentary defeat, demonstrating that the government's dominance in the Commons typically prevents defeats. Even a small government majority can exert significant control over legislative outcomes.

Structural challenges to representation

Parliament's structural limitations exacerbate its shortcomings. The first-past-the-post electoral system regularly distorts the relationship between votes cast and seats won, leaving millions of voters under-represented and an inability of Parliament to declare itself the legitimate voice of the electorate.

In 2024:
- The Labour Party secured 63% of seats with just 33% of the vote.
- Reform UK's 4.1 million votes (14.3%) secured them just five MPs (under 1% of the total).

Select committees, a key forum for scrutiny and representation, offer a partial remedy by allowing MPs to investigate issues beyond party lines. For example, the Education Select Committee's 2025 inquiry into teacher shortages reflects Parliament's capacity to represent long-term public concerns. However, these committees are made up in similar proportion to the Commons, they remain underfunded and overshadowed by expectations of party loyally.

Box 8.9 Examples of select committee activity in 2024

- **The Environmental Audit Committee** scrutinised the government's climate policies in 2024, recommending stronger emissions targets. While their report raised important issues, its influence was limited as the government maintained its existing commitments without substantial changes.
- The **Home Affairs Committee** conducted a 2024 inquiry into policing practices, suggesting reforms to enhance accountability and community relations. Despite highlighting critical issues, the government's

response was weak, demonstrating the challenges of implementing meaningful changes in a contentious political landscape.

- The **Health and Social Care Committee** examined the funding crisis in the NHS in 2024, calling for increased investment and better resource allocation. Though their recommendations were well received, the government's fiscal constraints hindered the implementation of any significant reforms.

Chapter summary: how effective is Parliament in performing its main functions?

Factor	Effective	Ineffective	Example
Structure of Commons and Lords	The division between the elected Commons and the unelected Lords allows for thorough scrutiny and expert input.	The unelected nature of the Lords limits public trust and accountability.	The House of Lords amended the Rwanda Asylum and Immigration Bill in 2024, refining its provisions before the Commons rejected them.
Powers of Commons and Lords	The Commons' supremacy in law-making ensures decisive action, while Lords offer a revising and delaying role.	The Lords' limited veto powers reduce their capacity to block legislation.	The Public Order Bill 2024 faced significant scrutiny in the Lords, but ultimately passed unchanged in the Commons.
Legislative process	The stages of bills, including readings and committee scrutiny, provide robust examination of legislation.	Amendments can be rejected by the Commons, limiting the Lords' influence.	The Children's Welfare Bill amendment in January 2025 saw opposition and amendments ignored, revealing the limits of their influence.

Parliament-executive relationship	Lords' independence forces ministers to justify actions, enhancing accountability.	The government's dominance in the Commons weakens parliamentary scrutiny.	The Public Health Bill 2024 faced significant pushback in the Lords, challenging government policies effectively.
Expertise and scrutiny	Lords' composition with diverse expertise improves detailed examination of bills.	Party dominance in the Commons reduces MPs' independence and expert input.	The Levelling-Up and Regeneration Bill 2024 saw over 1,000 amendments proposed by the Lords, reflecting their expertise.
Agenda-setting	The Lords address long-term policy issues like public health and climate change that the Commons may overlook.	Commons' short-term focus on election strategies limits long-term policy focus.	The Public Services Committee in 2024 raised awareness on post-pandemic mental health, driving government action.
Weak opposition	In times of weak Commons opposition, Lords serve as an effective check on government.	Weakness of the Conservative opposition reduces effective scrutiny in the Commons.	The House of Lords challenged the Public Health Bill more effectively than the weakened Commons opposition.
Select committees	Committees like the Education and Health conduct in-depth investigations into public concerns.	Party loyalties and limited resources undermine committee effectiveness.	The Environmental Audit Committee's scrutiny of climate policies in 2024 led to critical recommendations, though they had limited impact.

Representation issues	The FPTP system distorts representation, under-representing millions of voters.	Many voters feel their voices are not adequately represented.	In the 2024 election, Labour won 63% of seats with only 33% of the vote, highlighting vote-seat discrepancies.
Individual MPs' influence	Party discipline through the three-line whip curtails MPs' independence.	MPs often prioritise party loyalty over constituents' interests.	The Victims and Prisoners Bill amendment in December 2023 saw a rare defeat for the government due to cross-party efforts.

Conclusion

The UK Parliament's representative function in 2025 is constrained by systemic issues such as disproportional electoral outcomes, a dominant executive, weak opposition and the diminished independence of individual MPs. While Parliament retains mechanisms like select committees to address public concerns, its effectiveness as a representative institution is undermined by party discipline and electoral distortions. To enhance representation, reforms such as proportional representation and empowering MPs to vote more freely on contentious issues should be considered. Without such changes, Parliament risks alienating the diverse electorate it exists to serve.

Examination success

Sample essay examination questions:

- 'The House of Lords enhances the UK's democracy.' Analyse and evaluate this statement. (AQA-style, 25 marks)
- Evaluate the view that the House of Lords enhances the UK's democracy. (Edexcel-style, 30 marks)

Examiner's advice:

- Start by clearly explaining the House of Lords' functions, such as scrutiny, revising legislation and holding the government accountable. Explain how the House of Lords is the second chamber in the UK

Parliament and has distinct and lesser functions to the House of Commons.

- Critically assess both the positive and negative impacts of the House of Lords on democracy, using examples like its influence on key legislation, committee activity, scrutiny of government conduct and the extent of its legitimacy (its expertise and experience versus its unelected nature).
- Support your evaluation with specific case studies, such as amendments made to legislation and committee scrutiny that either strengthen or weaken democracy.

CHAPTER 9

Why have recent prime ministers and their cabinets struggled so much to dictate events and determine policy?

What you need to know

- In the UK, the prime minister, supported by the Cabinet, holds significant influence over both domestic and foreign policy decisions. This includes setting legislative agendas, responding to crises and guiding the direction of government. However, the effectiveness of this power often depends on party unity, parliamentary support and public perception.

- Recent UK prime ministers have faced numerous challenges, including party division, economic uncertainty, Brexit-related tensions and regional discontent. These issues have hampered their ability to maintain stable leadership, pass legislation and effectively manage crises.

- Key examples, such as Theresa May's handling of Brexit or Boris Johnson's response to the COVID-19 pandemic, provide crucial insights into the successes and failures of recent leaders. These examples can serve as valuable references for understanding the political complexities they navigated.

- Unlike the more constrained US presidency, the UK prime minister operates within a parliamentary system, requiring party support and parliamentary backing to govern effectively. The UK prime minister's power is shaped by parliamentary confidence, whereas the US president has more constitutional independence but less direct control over legislative outcomes.

Why have prime ministers and cabinets struggled since 2015

Traditionally the debate within British politics has been the extent to which prime ministers have been able to behave presidentially. However, since 2015, predominantly Conservative prime ministers and their cabinets have struggled to dictate events and to govern. Prime ministers with big majorities (Johnson, Truss, Sunak and more recently Starmer) struggling just as much as those with small majorities (Cameron and May).

For political commentator Anthony Seldon this is due to a combination of the following factors:

o Hubris (excessive pride or self-confidence)
o A lack of moral seriousness
o Internal infighting
o A lack of an achievable and clear agenda
o Inexperience, poor communication and judgement.

These failings have been exacerbated by the UK facing a succession of the challenges which have tested the capabilities of modern prime ministers:

• The aftermath of the financial crisis in 2008
• The UK's changing relationship with the European Union
• The COVID-19 crisis and its economic consequences
• The immigration crisis.

Table 9.1: The reasons why post 2010 Prime Ministers have struggled.

Prime Minister	Hubris	A lack of moral seriousness	Internal infighting	A lack of a clear and achievable agenda	A lack of experience, communication and judgement.
David Cameron	*		*		*
Theresa May	*		*	*	*
Boris Johnson	*	*	*	*	*
Liz Truss	*			*	*
Rishi Sunak			*	*	*
Keir Starmer	*			*	*

David Cameron 2010–2016

If David Cameron had lost the 2015 general election he would probably be remembered as a broadly successful prime minister. Coming to power in 2010 during the immediate aftermath of the financial crisis, his coalition government brought relative economic and political stability. However, it was hubris and a lack of judgement that caused his eventual downfall. Cameron called a referendum on the UK's membership of the EU to pacify the ideological splits in his party in the run-up to the 2015 general election, where he won with a small majority.

While he won the election, he lost the EU referendum after leading a flawed and disjointed Remain campaign. Rather than selling a positive vision of the EU, Cameron preferred to scare the electorate into staying, arguing that voting Leave would plunge the economy into a recession. Cameron seemed to concede that while the EU was a flawed institution, Britain would be worse off without it. Nigel Farage, one of the leaders of the Leave campaign, offered a positive vision for Britain if it left the UK, which ultimately proved more persuasive.

Cameron's failure to dictate events and policy was laid bare by the referendum defeat, moreover he was forced to suspend collective responsibility for his Cabinet during the referendum campaign as leading figures such as Boris Johnson campaigned for Leave. This Cabinet disunity would become a theme that would plague his immediate successors.

Theresa May (2016–2019)

Intense divisions within her party over the precise terms of the UK's exit from the EU presented Theresa May with the formidable challenge of uniting her party around a cohesive policy. In June 2017, she called a snap election, hoping to secure a substantial majority and enhance her legitimacy as she entered the Brexit negotiations. However, this decision backfired dramatically, leading to a net loss of 13 seats and the loss of her overall majority.

May was guilty of a mixture of poor judgement and communication:
  o May relied too much on a group of small advisers, chiefly Nick Timothy and Fiona Hall.
  o May's robotic campaign style and reliance on the phrase 'strong and stable' did not resonate well with the electorate.
  o The Conservative manifesto alienated her core support by a controversial funding change to caring for elderly people. Dubbed the 'dementia tax', it proved extremely unpopular.

Without an overall majority, Theresa May governed through a confidence and supply agreement with the Democratic Unionist Party (DUP). From the outset, it was a struggle; internal infighting within her party and Cabinet regarding the nature of the Brexit agreement led to a tumultuous premiership.

May faced two significant defeats as her own party rebelled against her, culminating in a historic loss of 230 votes on a Brexit agreement – the largest defeat for a sitting government in history. The principle of cabinet collective responsibility effectively collapsed over Brexit, resulting in 60 ministerial departures during her tenure, with 42 resignations stemming from discord over the issue.

May never fully recovered from the 2017 general election result, which revealed signs of hubris and overconfidence in her campaign strategy. Lacking a sizable majority, she struggled to exert control over both her Cabinet and her party, failing to articulate a clear Brexit deal that could unite them. Consequently, she found it impossible to dictate events and set policy. Chief Whip Julian Smith described May's Cabinet as exhibiting the "worst cabinet ill-discipline in history".

Comparing the differences between the UK prime minister and the US president

The UK prime minister and the US president both act as heads of government, leading their respective political parties and initiating legislation. They play vital roles during times of crisis, serving as national figureheads to steer their countries through significant events. However, their powers and structures differ markedly. The US president is both the head of state and the head of government, possessing exclusive powers such as signing and vetoing legislation, appointing federal judges, and granting pardons. In contrast, the UK prime minister functions within a parliamentary system, where the monarch serves as the head of state, and key powers, such as judicial appointments, reside with the Judicial Appointments Commission.

Term limits further differentiate the two roles; the president is limited to two terms, while the prime minister has no such constraints. The US system emphasises separation of powers, often resulting in legislative gridlock, whereas the UK's fusion of powers typically enables the prime minister to pass legislation more easily. Additionally, the president's Executive Office provides substantial support, while the prime minister relies on a smaller staff and the Cabinet. Ultimately, while both leaders navigate domestic and international challenges, their operational frameworks and powers reflect their distinct political systems.

Boris Johnson (2019–2022)

Johnson's snap election in December 2019 saw him run a very successful campaign, winning a landslide victory with a majority of 80 seats and receiving 43.6% of the popular vote – the highest percentage for any party since the 1979 general election. Unlike May, Johnson was able to articulate a clear agenda, promising to "get Brexit done". Having achieved a Brexit deal and with the party united around him, Johnson seemed impregnable.

However, the COVID crisis saw both Johnson and his Cabinet struggle to dictate events. Johnson's lack of seriousness, poor work ethic and leadership skills led to difficulties during the crisis. Anthony Seldon described a chaotic inner sanctum, with Johnson heavily dependent upon his chief adviser, Dominic Cummings, who, for a time, assumed almost universal power over the Cabinet as the pandemic unfolded.

The failure of Johnson and his inner circle to follow lockdown regulations caused him to lose the support of his backbenchers and ministers over allegations that he had misled Parliament regarding lockdown breaches. In early July 2022, there were mass resignations, including five Cabinet ministers and 25 other ministers. This hubris and lack of judgement from Johnson led to an unprecedented collapse of his government, despite a sizable working majority.

Liz Truss (2022)

With a sizeable working majority and the worst of COVID behind the country, Liz Truss, the new prime minister, had a platform to rebuild. She lasted 44 days due to one hubristic event: the September 2022 'mini-budget'. Chancellor Kwasi Kwarteng's plans for £45 billion of unfunded tax cuts led to a horrified reaction from investors as the pound fell to its lowest ever level against the dollar, and gilt prices collapsed amid panic over the implications of the mini-budget.

To address the financial crisis:

- Truss dismissed Kwarteng from his role as chancellor.
- She was forced to endure the humiliation of hearing her new chancellor, Jeremy Hunt, critique and reverse the mini-budget to placate the financial markets.
- Ultimately, Truss resigned following a total breakdown of support from both Parliament and the grassroots party.

The mini-budget was a self-inflicted disaster that demonstrated a lack of experience and judgement on Truss and Kwarteng's part.

Rishi Sunak (2022–24)

Rishi Sunak faced a cost-of-living crisis with soaring inflation, an NHS overwhelmed by pandemic backlogs and seasonal illnesses, and an immigration crisis marked by rising illegal crossings and complex asylum processes, all compounded by global geopolitical tensions.

While Sunak had a clear vision and a plan in the form of five pledges, he and his government struggled to deliver.

How successful were Sunak's five pledges?

• Halve inflation within a year

Inflation measured by the consumer price index did fall to 2.3% by April 2024, however this was primarily due to global factors, particularly falling energy prices so it was difficult for Sunak to claim direct credit.

• Grow the economy

The UK economy grew modestly, with GDP expected to rise about 0.5% in 2023, partly due to upward revisions for 2021 and 2022. Sunak and his chancellor, Jeremy Hunt, deserve credit for policies boosting investment, but outside factors and low productivity growth – averaging just 1.1% since 2010 – greatly affected economic performance.

- **Reduce national debt**

Public sector net debt rose from 85.1% to 88.3% of GDP from December 2022 to November 2023. Sunak faced the dual problem of trying to grow the economy and cut spending.

- **Cut NHS waiting lists**

Sunak failure to reduce waiting times stemmed from multiple challenges: soaring inflation increased operational costs, while ongoing strikes forced the NHS to pay more for temporary staff, further straining finances. The government could only allocate £100 million of the requested £1.2 billion due to budget constraints and competing financial pressures, limiting resources.

- **Stop small boats**

Despite the government's efforts, nearly 30,000 migrants crossed in 2023, indicating that the issue remains significant. Additionally, the plan to send migrants to Rwanda faced legal hurdles, including a Supreme Court ruling that deemed Rwanda unsafe, complicating removal processes. Many provisions of the Illegal Migration Act 2023 also remain unimplemented due to a lack of safe countries to which migrants can be sent.

Sunak's gamble to call an early election backfired

Sunak's decision to call an early election had a presidential quality, as he bypassed consultation with his Cabinet, resulting in a disastrous defeat in the July election. This misjudgement significantly limited his ability to capitalise on potential gains, such as decreasing inflation and effective policy implementations, which could have enhanced public support and strengthened the Conservative Party's position.

Has the role of prime minister become an impossible job?

Sir Anthony Seldon believes that prime ministers are struggling due to several interconnected factors. First, recent leaders have faced unprecedented challenges, particularly related to Brexit, which has caused instability and division within the nation.

The short tenure of Liz Truss and Boris Johnson's sudden resignation are indicators of deeper issues within leadership. Seldon emphasises a lack of preparation, arguing that many recent prime ministers have not accumulated sufficient experience before taking office. For example, Rishi Sunak entered Parliament only in 2015, with limited ministerial roles, which sharply contrasts with past leaders who had extensive governmental experience. None of the current Labour front bench has any meaningful experience of working within the business community.

In his book, *The Impossible Office?*, Seldon states, "No one becomes head of an organisation knowing very little about how to do the job," underscoring the urgent need for better-prepared leaders in modern British politics.

Keir Starmer (2024–)

Since becoming prime minister, Sir Keir Starmer has struggled due to plummeting approval ratings, internal party conflicts and a lack of cohesive governance.

- o The UK economy saw only slight growth of 0.1% between July and September, as uncertainty surrounding the Budget played a role in this lacklustre performance. Labour aimed to enhance economic growth upon assuming office, but numerous businesses have voiced criticism of the tax increases in the Budget, arguing that they will result in higher prices and a decrease in new job opportunities.
- o Economic forecasts indicate sluggish growth despite increased public spending and borrowing, while reliance on state-driven initiatives instead of fostering private sector growth has drawn criticism, resulting in a disappointing start to his premiership.
- o Labour has alienated women and pensioners by implementing policies that reduce financial support, such as cutting winter fuel payments for millions, which disproportionately affects vulnerable groups. Additionally, the refusal to compensate women impacted by changes to the state pension age was seen as two-faced given his party's support for this issue while in opposition.
- o The controversy surrounding Sue Gray's appointment as chief of staff – having previously led investigations into party conduct – raised ethical concerns.
- o Additionally, Starmer faced criticism for accepting free gifts, which further damaged his credibility. Having previously condemned Boris Johnson's

regime for enjoying similar perks, his acceptance of gifts appeared hypocritical and insensitive, especially amid a cost-of-living crisis.

Chapter summary	Details
Why have recent prime ministers and their cabinets struggled so much to dictate events and determine policy?	Prime ministers in the UK, supported by the Cabinet, wield significant influence over domestic and foreign policy, but their effectiveness depends on party unity, parliamentary backing and public perception. Challenges such as party division, economic uncertainty, Brexit and regional discontent have hindered their leadership, making it difficult to set clear agendas and govern effectively.
David Cameron (2010–2016)	Cameron's coalition government brought economic and political stability, but hubris and a lack of judgement led to his downfall after the EU referendum. His leadership suffered due to a flawed campaign and internal disunity, showing his inability to dictate events and policy effectively.
Theresa May (2016–2019)	May struggled to unite her party around Brexit, which led to poor judgement and communication errors. Her loss of an overall majority and divisive leadership resulted in significant defeats and internal infighting, weakening her ability to set policy.
Boris Johnson (2019–2022)	Johnson's early success with a Brexit deal was overshadowed by his poor handling of the COVID-19 pandemic. His chaotic leadership, hubris and reliance on key advisors led to a loss of parliamentary support and eventual downfall despite a sizable majority.
Liz Truss (2022)	Truss's brief premiership was marred by the mini-budget, a lack of experience, poor judgement and hubris, leading to financial turmoil, Cabinet infighting and eventual resignation.
Rishi Sunak (2022–2024)	Sunak faced a series of crises – inflation, NHS backlogs, and immigration – but struggled to deliver on key pledges due to external factors, limited influence and misjudged electoral strategy.

Keir Starmer (2024–)	Starmer has struggled with weak economic performance, internal party conflicts and lack of clear governance, leading to falling approval ratings and ethical controversies.
Comparison with the US president	The UK prime minister operates within a parliamentary system, needing party support and parliamentary backing, while the US president has more constitutional independence but less direct legislative control. The UK system emphasises collective decision-making, whereas the US president has greater unilateral powers.

Conclusion

Since 2016, prime ministers and their cabinets have found it difficult to influence events and formulate policy. This struggle stems not only from the exceptionally challenging circumstances they have encountered but also from deficiencies in leadership and statecraft.

- Hubris has proven to be a significant weakness, leading to overconfidence and poor decision-making. Cameron's decision to risk EU membership – something he passionately supported for the sake of party unity – was misguided. Both May and Sunak made errors in calling elections, while Truss's handling of the mini-budget displayed remarkable arrogance.
- A lack of moral seriousness has further eroded public trust and accountability, particularly during the COVID crisis under Johnson. In opposition, Starmer was highly critical of Johnson for accepting free gifts; thus, his own acceptance of such gifts, along with those of his Cabinet, appeared politically naïve.
- Internal infighting has also obstructed coherent governance, especially during Theresa May's tenure, where divisive party dynamics created significant challenges.
- Moreover, the absence of a clear and achievable agenda has troubled leaders like Sunak and Starmer, who struggled to respond effectively to pressing issues such as the cost-of-living crisis and economic management.

Together, these factors have fostered a broader sense of instability within British politics, hindering recent prime ministers from successfully influencing events and shaping policy during extremely turbulent times.

Examination success

Examination-style questions:

- The modern prime minister has little opportunity to dictate policy, and even fewer opportunities to guarantee a successful outcome. Analyse and evaluate this statement. (25 marks, AQA style)
- Evaluate the view that since 1997 prime ministers always control the decisions made by their governments. (30 marks, Edexcel style)

Examiner's advice

- Ensure you have a clear grasp of the factors influencing prime ministerial power, including party unity, parliamentary support, external crises, economic pressures and leadership style. Focus on the limitations prime ministers face in controlling events and guaranteeing outcomes, while also considering the role of other actors (e.g. Cabinet members, MPs and the public).

- Utilise specific examples from recent prime ministers (Cameron, May, Johnson, Truss, Sunak and Starmer) to illustrate key points. Provide detailed evidence of successes and failures to substantiate your argument. Ensure your examples are well-chosen to clearly demonstrate the challenges faced by modern leaders in influencing policy outcomes.

- Balance your answer by considering both the constraints and opportunities available to prime ministers. Weigh the evidence carefully – acknowledge the circumstances where prime ministers have been able to exert control, but also highlight the frequent limits on their influence. This will allow you to critically evaluate the statement or question fully.

- Clearly state your own judgement on the degree of influence modern prime ministers have had on policy outcomes. Support this judgement with evidence and tie your analysis back to relevant political theories (e.g. the prime ministerial power thesis, collective responsibility and the role of Parliament). This will show a deeper understanding of the broader political context and strengthen your argument.

CHAPTER 10
The Supreme Court
Is the UK Supreme Court in 2025
an effective guardian of rights?

What you need to know

- The UK Supreme Court is the highest court in the United Kingdom. Its powers lie in reviewing, interpreting and applying the law, particularly in cases involving human rights, constitutional matters and disputes over devolution.

- As part of the judicial branch, the Supreme Court operates independently and separate from the executive and legislature. The security of tenure for justices and the appointment process for senior judges are designed to minimise political influence.

- Landmark Supreme Court cases in the last decade, such as *Miller v Secretary of State for Exiting the EU (2017)* and *R (Miller) v The Prime Minister (2019)*, have demonstrated the Court's role in addressing constitutional issues and holding the government to account.

- Debate continues on several counts. Is the judicial branch sufficiently independent? Is the Supreme Court an effective guardian of rights, considering its reliance on the Human Rights Act 1998 and its limitations in overturning legislation due to parliamentary sovereignty? Does the Supreme Court strike the right balance between activism and restraint.

The UK Supreme Court's power and influence have been debated extensively in recent years. For some, the Court's interpretative function plays too powerful a role in policymaking, dominating the executive and legislative branches. However, the UK's uncodified constitution and the lack of a complete separation of powers means that the sovereignty of Parliament – to make or unmake any law it chooses – remains a substantial check on the Supreme Court in the UK.

Box 10.1 Key definitions with recent examples [indented for example?]

- **Judicial review** is the process by which UK courts assess the lawfulness of decisions made by public bodies, ensuring they comply with the law and respect individual rights.
- **Judicial independence** is the principle that judges must remain free from external pressures, such as government influence or public opinion, ensuring impartiality and fairness in their decisions. The Supreme Court's 2024 decision on the Northern Ireland Protocol reaffirmed judicial independence by ruling against a government interpretation, despite political backlash.
- **Judicial activism** occurs when judges are perceived to go beyond the strict application of the law to influence public policy or address social issues.
- **Judicial restraint** is the principle where judges avoid making rulings that could be seen as creating or influencing policy, instead adhering strictly to legal interpretation.

How powerful is the UK Supreme Court in 2025?

Any contemporary analysis of Supreme Court power in the UK will draw on notable examples over the last decade, mostly concentrating on the relationship between the legal branch and the executive branch in the context of the UK's protracted exit from the European Union.

- In 2017's *R (Miller) v Secretary of State for Exiting the European Union*, the Court ruled that Prime Minister Theresa May could not trigger Article 50 without parliamentary approval, thereby restricting executive power.
- Similarly, in 2019's *R (Miller) v The Prime Minister*, the Court deemed Boris Johnson's prorogation of Parliament unlawful, enabling MPs to further scrutinise Brexit policies after Parliament was ordered to resume session.

Further to these, more recent rulings in the 2020s reflect the Supreme Court's continued influence and impact on political life:

- In *R (AAA (Syria) and others v Secretary of State for the Home Department (2023)*, the Court declared the government's plan to send asylum seekers to Rwanda unlawful, forcing legislative amendments through the Safety of Rwanda Act 2024.

- In July 2024, in *R (on the application of Finch on behalf of the Weald Action Group) 'Finch' v Surrey County Council and others*, the UK Supreme Court ruled that all fossil fuel projects must be assessed for their future environmental impact, a decision that went against government approvals of certain projects.

Yet, it is not all one way, and there are notable recent instances where the Supreme Court has supported the government:

- In *R (Begum) v Secretary of State for the Home Department (2021, reaffirmed in 2024)*, the Court upheld the government's decision to strip Shamima Begum of her citizenship, citing national security concerns.
- In July 2024, the Supreme Court ruled in *Lipton v BA Cityflyer Ltd (2024)* that airlines must compensate passengers for flights cancelled due to pilot illness, stating that such cancellations are not considered 'extraordinary circumstances'. This decision supported consumer rights but also aligned with existing government regulations aimed at protecting passengers.

Recent cases and judgements continue to highlight the power of the Court to both resist and support the UK executive and government. Cases and judgements illustrate the ongoing tension between the judiciary and government, fuelling debates over judicial overreach and while also reflecting the Court's deference to executive power in specific contexts.

Box 10.2 Comparison between the UK and US Supreme Courts – judicial independence in the 2020s

The independence of the judiciary in the UK is safeguarded by the Constitutional Reform Act 2005, which separates the judiciary from the legislative and executive branches. Judges are appointed by independent commissions, and their neutrality is emphasised in decisions that avoid overt political commentary.

- *In the 2024 Northern Ireland Protocol case, the UK Supreme Court upheld the legality of the protocol arrangements, which was viewed as a neutral decision supporting neither political side in post-Brexit politics.*

While judicial independence is similarly constitutionally enshrined, US justices are nominated by the president and confirmed by the Senate. These arrangements often lead to perceptions of politicisation based on ideological leanings. Lifetime appointments also mean that the court's composition may reflect past administrations' political priorities.

- *Dispute arose when the Dobbs v. Jackson Women's Health Organization (2022) decision continued to influence state abortion laws in 2024, with the Court's conservative majority seen as influencing policies aligned with Republican values, highlighting perceptions of partisanship in the US judiciary.*

The UK Supreme Court in 2025 – activist or restrained?

Throughout the 2020s, the UK Supreme Court has continued to deliver rulings that run the full range: reinforcing judicial authority; supporting government legislation; challenging the extent of the powers of elected officials; prompting criticism over perceived policymaking. 2024 saw no explicit diminishment of Court power, yet its decisions continued to spark debates about its influence on legislative processes and executive actions.

Box 10.3 Judicial activism – case studies

The Manchester Ship Canal Company Ltd v United Utilities Water Plc (2024)

In *The Manchester Ship Canal Company Ltd v United Utilities Water Plc (2024)*, the UK Supreme Court unanimously ruled that the Canal Company could pursue claims of nuisance or trespass against United Utilities for unauthorised sewage discharges into the canal.

This decision overturned previous lower court rulings that had favoured United Utilities, thereby reinforcing property rights and environmental protections. Legal experts noted that the judgement could lead to substantial compensation payouts and motivate infrastructure investments to prevent sewage spills.

The Court's willingness to challenge established statutory interpretations and support private claims against a utility company exemplifies judicial activism, as it actively shaped legal precedents to address contemporary environmental concerns.

> ### QX v Secretary of State for the Home Department (2024)
>
> QX, a British citizen, resided in Syria from 2014 to 2018. Upon deportation from Turkey in 2018, the Home Secretary imposed a temporary exclusion order (TEO) on him, suspecting involvement with an al-Qaeda-aligned group. QX contested the TEO, seeking disclosure of the evidence underpinning the Home Secretary's decision.
>
> The Court unanimously ruled against the Home Secretary, saying that the Home Secretary must provide QX with adequate disclosure of the evidence supporting the allegations, to enable him to challenge governmental decisions effectively.
>
> This judgement exemplifies judicial activism, where the Court actively interprets legal provisions to uphold individual rights. This proactive stance emphasises the judiciary's role in scrutinising executive actions, particularly in national security contexts, to safeguard civil liberties.

Rulings in 2024 have therefore reignited debates about judicial overreach. Critics argue that rulings against the government and government ministers – such as those delivered in the cases involving The Manchester Ship Canal and Syrian national 'QX' – are examples of a creeping 'kritarchy' (from the Ancient Greek meaning 'rule by judges') where unelected judges dictate policy decisions instead of reflecting the electorate's will. Yet supporters of these decisions see a Court merely prepared to uphold common law, civil and human rights.

Box 10.4 Judicial restraint – case studies

> ### M (Belarus) v Secretary of State for the Home Department (2024)
>
> AM, a Belarusian national, lived in the UK for 26 years without legal status after obstructing his removal by falsely denying his nationality. His prolonged undocumented status and criminal offences prevented him from gaining leave to remain through normal routes. AM argued that his situation violated his human rights under Article 8 of the European Convention on Human Rights (ECHR), which guarantees the right to private and family life.
>
> This ruling exemplifies judicial restraint by upholding the government's immigration policy rather than expanding rights for individuals who

undermine legal frameworks. The Court refrained from imposing broader human rights obligations that could incentivise obstructive behaviour, prioritising public confidence in immigration controls over individual claims.

For Women Scotland v The Lord Advocate (2024)

For Women Scotland v The Lord Advocate (2024) revolved around the interpretation of 'woman' in the Gender Representation on Public Boards (Scotland) Act 2018. For Women Scotland argued that the inclusion of transgender women with Gender Recognition Certificates (GRCs) in the act's definition of 'woman' contradicted the Equality Act 2010. They contended that 'woman' should exclusively refer to biological females, ensuring protections for sex-based rights. The Scottish government maintained that individuals legally recognised as female under the Gender Recognition Act 2004 should be included in the definition.

The Supreme Court upheld the Scottish government's position, affirming that the inclusion of transgender women with GRCs aligns with the legislative intent of both the 2004 Act and the Equality Act. The ruling emphasised that the act's purpose was to increase diversity without undermining existing protections.

The Court's decision is an example of judicial restraint, as it deferred to the legislative intent and avoided setting a precedent that could undermine existing legal frameworks. By respecting parliamentary sovereignty, the Court limited its role to clarifying the compatibility of laws rather than imposing broader interpretations or policy changes.

The events of 2024 demonstrate the UK Supreme Court's complex relationship with the executive and legislature. While Court rulings continue to shape public policy and legislative processes, accusations of judicial overreach persist. That said, the principle of parliamentary sovereignty and the UK's uncodified constitution prevent the Court from becoming as powerful as its counterparts in countries like the United States. The ongoing debate about the Court's role underscores the delicate balance between judicial independence, policymaking and democratic accountability.

Is the Supreme Court an effective guardian of civil liberties?

Yes, it regularly upholds liberties

The UK Supreme Court has proven effective in safeguarding civil liberties, particularly when government policies risk breaching established human rights standards. Its rulings often challenge executive overreach, ensuring accountability and compliance with the European Convention on Human Rights (ECHR). In *R (on the application of Smith) v Secretary of State for the Home Department (2024)*, the Court ruled that using repurposed barge housing for asylum seekers violated Article 3 of the ECHR, which prohibits inhuman or degrading treatment. This decision highlighted the Court's ability to defend fundamental human rights and hold the government accountable for policies that contravene international obligations.

No, it is reluctant to intervene in socio-economic issues

The Supreme Court's capacity to protect rights is less effective when addressing socio-economic issues, often seen as matters of political discretion. In *R (on the application of Jones) v HM Treasury (2024)*, the Court upheld the government's decision to limit energy support payments, reasoning that such economic policies fall under Parliament's remit. This highlights a gap in judicial oversight where socio-economic rights are concerned, leaving vulnerable groups without robust protections. The Court's reluctance to intervene reflects the weaker legal standing of socio-economic rights compared to civil and political rights.

Yes, it affirms workers' and privacy rights

The Court has actively supported key rights like workers' protections and privacy safeguards, stepping in where legal gaps exist. In *Mercer v Alternative Futures Group (2024)*, the Court ruled that denying strike-related protections under section 146 of the Trade Union Labour Relations (Consolidation) Act 1992 was incompatible with Article 11 of the ECHR. This landmark judgement protected workers from detrimental treatment short of dismissal, affirming the fundamental right to strike. Similarly, in privacy cases, the Court has scrutinised government surveillance measures, reinforcing its role in defending against state overreach.

No, it is constrained by constitutional circumstances

The Supreme Court's institutional limitations, rooted in the UK's uncodified constitution, restrict its effectiveness as a guardian of rights. Unlike courts in jurisdictions with codified constitutions, it cannot strike down legislation outright and must rely on declarations of incompatibility under the Human Rights Act. In *R (on the application of Digital Privacy UK) v Home Office (2024)*, the Court found parts of the Investigatory Powers Act 2016 incompatible with Article 8 of the ECHR but left the remedy to Parliament. This structural constraint reduces the judiciary's ability to enforce rights directly, making protection dependent on political will.

Chapter summary: evidence and evaluation

Case	Role and powers	Judicial independence	Effectiveness in protecting rights
R (Finch) v Surrey County Council (2024)	Required Surrey County Council to consider global environmental impacts of local oil production decisions.	Showcased independence by ruling against government-backed industrial policies, maintaining impartiality.	Highlighted the Court's role in enforcing environmental rights, though critics argued it ventured into policymaking.
Manchester Ship Canal Co. v United Utilities (2024)	Ruled water companies could be sued for raw sewage dumping, affirming common law rights over statutory interpretation.	Demonstrated judicial independence by challenging corporate practices under common law protections.	Bolstered environmental and property rights, receiving public approval due to concerns over water pollution.
R (Smith) v Secretary of State for Home Department (2024)	Struck down barge housing for asylum seekers as violating Article 3 of the ECHR (inhuman or degrading treatment).	Asserted independence by challenging a government policy linked to sensitive political issues.	Highlighted effectiveness in safeguarding human rights, though practical enforcement depends on political will.

R (Jones) v HM Treasury (2024)	Upheld government decision limiting energy support payments, emphasising economic policy falls under Parliament.	Respected judicial independence by adhering to the separation of powers in economic policymaking.	Exposed limits in protecting socio-economic rights due to parliamentary sovereignty and lack of explicit protections.
R (Digital Privacy UK) v Home Office (2024)	Declared parts of the Investigatory Powers Act 2016 incompatible with Article 8 ECHR (right to privacy).	Maintained independence by scrutinising government surveillance measures for proportionality and safeguards.	Protected privacy rights effectively, ensuring government compliance with human rights standards.

Conclusion

The power of the UK Supreme Court is nuanced, reflecting a delicate balance between judicial activism and restraint. Advocates of judicial activism argue that the Court plays a crucial role in safeguarding individual rights and upholding the rule of law, as seen in landmark cases like Miller, where it asserted its authority to check executive power. These decisions exemplify the Court's commitment to protecting citizens' rights against potential governmental overreach.

Conversely, there are instances of judicial restraint, where the Court has been cautious not to overstep its bounds. For example, in cases concerning parliamentary sovereignty, the Supreme Court has often refrained from interfering too deeply in legislative matters, thereby reinforcing the principle of parliamentary supremacy.

Ultimately, while the Supreme Court undeniably wields significant influence in shaping UK law and protecting rights, it does so within a framework that respects the authority of Parliament. This balance is essential to maintaining a functional democracy, ensuring that neither branch overreaches its powers.

Examination success

Sample essay examination questions:

- 'The Judiciary has a significant impact on the government and policymaking processes in the UK'. Analyse and evaluate this statement. (AQA style, 25 marks)
- Evaluate the view that the UK Supreme Court now has too much influence over the legislative and policymaking processes. (Edexcel style, 30 marks)

Examiner's advice:

- Begin with a strong, concise thesis statement that directly addresses the question. Clearly outline your argument and the main points you will discuss. This will guide your analysis and help structure your response effectively, ensuring you stay focused on the question throughout.
- Support your analysis with specific, contemporary examples of judicial decisions and their impacts on government and policymaking. This demonstrates your knowledge of recent developments and illustrates how the judiciary interacts with other branches of government, enhancing your evaluation of the statement.
- In your evaluation, consider and weigh multiple viewpoints. Discuss arguments for and against the influence of the judiciary on legislation, assessing the implications of cases like Miller, Finch and Begum. This critical approach reflects your analytical skills and depth of understanding, earning higher marks.
- Integrate relevant political concepts and theories, such as the separation of powers, judicial review and the rule of law. Explain how these concepts relate to your argument and the questions posed, demonstrating a comprehensive understanding of the political framework and the judiciary's role within it.

STUDENT QUESTIONS

Make notes in response to the following questions. Use the information in this book, other textbooks and class notes.

Chapter 1 – Democracy and participation

1. What are the key features of representative democracy in the UK, and how does it differ from direct democracy?
2. How does low voter turnout impact the legitimacy of UK governments, and what specific examples illustrate this challenge?
3. In what ways has declining political party membership affected UK democracy, and what are some of the main reasons for this trend?
4. What role do trust and alienation play in the perceived participation crisis in the UK, and how do they manifest in public attitudes toward government?
5. How have alternative forms of participation, such as protests and online activism, supplemented or replaced traditional political engagement in the UK?
6. What evidence is there that younger people are more politically engaged than previous generations, and how do they participate differently?
7. What arguments exist against the idea of a participation crisis in the UK, and how do they counter the evidence of declining turnout and party membership?
8. How do non-traditional forms of political participation, such as online activism and issue-based movements, present both opportunities and limitations for democratic engagement in the UK?

Chapter 2 – Party systems

1. What are the key characteristics of a two-party system, and how have Labour and the Conservatives exemplified these in UK politics over the last century?
2. Explain how the first-past-the-post (FPTP) electoral system has historically supported the dominance of the two main parties. What evidence suggests this trend is now under pressure?

3. What evidence from the 2024 general election supports the argument that the UK is moving toward a multiparty system?
4. How do the performances of minor parties, such as the Liberal Democrats and Reform UK, demonstrate the limitations and opportunities within the FPTP electoral system?
5. Discuss the role of voter volatility in the potential decline of the two-party system. How has this been evident in recent elections, particularly in 2024?
6. What structural barriers, such as electoral geography and tactical voting, prevent the Liberal Democrats from achieving greater success under the FPTP system?
7. Using the example of Reform UK, assess how the rise of new political forces could challenge the Labour–Conservative duopoly in the UK.
8. In what ways do devolved governments in the UK (e.g. Scotland, Wales) exemplify multiparty politics, and what impact has this had on Westminster politics?

Chapter 3 – Electoral systems and first-past-the-post

1. What are the traditional strengths of FPTP that have made it the dominant electoral system in the UK for over 80 years?
2. How did the 2024 general election result reflect FPTP's effectiveness in delivering stable government and clear mandates?
3. Critically assess the impact of FPTP on smaller parties, using the 2024 election as an example.
4. In what ways does FPTP contribute to voter disillusionment and low turnout, particularly in safe seats?
5. Compare the electoral outcomes produced by FPTP in the 2019 and 2024 general elections. How do these results demonstrate FPTP's strengths and weaknesses?
6. Evaluate the claim that FPTP's simplicity and efficiency come at the cost of proportional representation.
7. How does FPTP compare to other electoral systems in the UK, such as the Additional Member System (AMS) and the Single Transferable Vote (STV)?
8. Do you think FPTP's ability to produce strong, single-party governments outweighs the criticisms surrounding its disproportional outcomes? Justify your answer.

Chapter 4 – Voting behaviour

1. Explain how class-based voting has historically influenced UK elections. How did this pattern shift in the 2024 general election?
2. What is dealignment, and how did it affect Labour and Conservative voting patterns between 2019 and 2024?
3. Discuss the role of age in shaping voting behaviour in the 2024 UK general election. Which demographic groups leaned towards Labour and which towards the Conservatives?
4. How does positional theory help explain Labour's victory in 2024? Provide examples from the 2024 campaign that illustrate this theory.
5. Describe the impact of Reform UK on the Conservative vote in 2024. How did this differ from its role in 2019?
6. Discuss the significance of valence theory in understanding the outcomes of the 2024 UK general election. How did Labour's leadership and party competence play a role?
7. What was the role of educational attainment in voting behaviour in 2024? How did voters with and without degrees differ in their support for Labour and the Conservatives?
8. Explain why turnout was historically low in the 2024 general election. What factors contributed to voter apathy, and how did this impact the election outcome?

Chapter 5 – Media influence

1. Explain the different ways in which traditional media and social media influenced voter perceptions during the 2024 UK general election.
2. Analyse the role of social media in shaping voter behaviour and mobilising political engagement in the 2024 UK general election.
3. Evaluate the effectiveness of traditional media compared to social media in reaching different voter groups in the 2024 election.
4. Discuss how media bias manifested in the 2024 UK general election and its impact on voter perceptions. Provide specific examples.
5. How did artificial intelligence (AI) influence the 2024 UK general election campaigns? Discuss the advantages and potential risks of AI in political messaging.
6. Compare the use of social media in the UK election with its use in the US presidential election of 2024. How did media strategies differ between the two countries?

7. Examine the impact of micro-targeting in political campaigns using AI tools in the 2024 UK general election.
8. Discuss the role of legacy media outlets like newspapers and television in shaping public discourse, even with the rise of digital platforms.

Chapter 6 – The UK constitution

1. What are the main features of the UK's uncodified constitution, and how do they differ from those of a codified constitution?
2. How does Labour's approach to devolution within England differ from previous governments, and what challenges might arise in its implementation?
3. Discuss the potential benefits and limitations of Labour's plan to strengthen intergovernmental cooperation through the Council of the Nations and Regions.
4. Analyse Labour's proposed House of Lords reform, focusing on the removal of hereditary peers and the plan to establish an 'Assembly of Nations and Regions'.
5. To what extent could Labour's devolution proposals for Scotland, Wales and Northern Ireland strengthen the Union? Consider the impact of constitutional safeguards and new powers.
6. Evaluate the ethical reforms proposed by Labour, including the establishment of an Independent Integrity and Ethics Commission and revisions to the Ministerial Code.
7. What are the economic and political implications of Labour's plan to decentralise civil service roles and empower regional mayors?
8. Assess the feasibility and potential impact of Labour's overall constitutional reform agenda on improving democratic accountability and public trust in UK politics.

Chapter 7 – Devolution

1. Define devolution and explain how it differs from federalism, using examples from the UK and the USA.
2. Explain the role and impact of metro mayors in England, citing examples from Greater Manchester and London.
3. Discuss the successes of devolution in promoting regional legislation that supports national distinctiveness, referencing recent acts in Scotland and Wales.

4. Assess the extent to which devolution has preserved the unity of the UK. What role has devolution played in managing nationalist pressures?
5. Analyse the challenges facing devolution in Northern Ireland, with reference to Brexit and political instability.
6. Examine the criticisms of economic disparities under devolution, with a focus on Scotland's productivity issues. How have these disparities impacted the overall effectiveness of devolution?
7. Compare and contrast the COVID-19 pandemic response and COP26 as examples of cross-border cooperation within the UK under the devolved framework.
8. Outline and assess three potential strategies for the future of devolution in the UK. Which strategy, if any, do you believe is the most viable?

Chapter 8 – Parliament

1. Explain the key differences between the House of Commons and the House of Lords in terms of their composition, roles and powers.
2. How do the Parliament Acts of 1911 and 1949 limit the powers of the House of Lords? Provide examples.
3. Evaluate the role of the Salisbury Convention in maintaining the democratic mandate of the House of Commons.
4. Discuss the stages of the legislative process in the UK Parliament and assess their effectiveness in scrutinising and passing legislation.
5. To what extent does the House of Lords improve the quality of legislation? Use examples such as the amendments to the Rwanda Asylum and Immigration Bill or the Public Order Bill.
6. Examine the strengths and weaknesses of select committees in holding the government accountable. Use specific examples from 2024.
7. What impact did the 2024 UK general election have on Parliament's ability to perform its representative and legislative functions?
8. Analyse the role of individual MPs in representing constituents and scrutinising the government. How does party discipline, such as three-line whips, affect their independence?

Chapter 9 – Prime minister and Cabinet

1. What role does party unity play in the Prime Minister's ability to dictate events and determine policy? Provide examples from recent premierships.
2. Why was hubris a significant factor in the downfalls of David Cameron and Liz Truss?
3. How did infighting within the Conservative Party affect Theresa May's ability to lead effectively?
4. Discuss how external crises such as the COVID-19 pandemic and the cost-of-living crisis impacted Boris Johnson and Rishi Sunak's leadership.
5. Compare and contrast the challenges faced by Theresa May and Boris Johnson in managing their cabinets.
6. Why has the lack of a clear and achievable agenda been a recurring issue for UK prime ministers since 2015?
7. To what extent does the parliamentary system in the UK hinder the prime minister's ability to act decisively, compared to the US president?
8. How have ethical controversies, such as those faced by Boris Johnson and Keir Starmer, influenced public trust and the effectiveness of their leadership?

Chapter 10 – the UK Supreme Court

1. What is the role of the UK Supreme Court in safeguarding human rights, and how does it interpret the law in this capacity?
2. How does the principle of parliamentary sovereignty limit the UK Supreme Court's power in protecting individual rights?
3. Explain the significance of judicial independence in the UK, using examples of recent Supreme Court cases to illustrate this concept.
4. Compare and contrast the powers of the UK Supreme Court with those of the US Supreme Court, focusing on judicial independence and the separation of powers.
5. What is judicial review, and how has the UK Supreme Court used this power in cases such as R (Miller) v Secretary of State for Exiting the EU (2017)?
6. How do recent cases like R (Finch) v Surrey County Council (2024) highlight the tension between judicial activism and judicial restraint in the UK Supreme Court?

7. Evaluate the effectiveness of the UK Supreme Court as a guardian of civil liberties, using examples of recent decisions such as R (Smith) v Secretary of State for Home Department (2024).
8. What are the key arguments for and against the perception of 'judicial overreach' in the UK Supreme Court, as illustrated by recent landmark cases?

Printed in Great Britain
by Amazon